When Ties Unbind

MATTIE WARD

When Ties Unbind

MATTIE WARD

ISBN 13: 979-8-9874661-0-0

First Printing: December 2022

Printed in the United States of America

10 9 8 7 6 5 4 3 2 1

Dedication

Charlotte Valencia Banks

December 23, 1966 – May 25, 2006

To my baby girl:

I dedicate this book in your honor. It was your manuscript that was the start of my journey. With God's Grace, His favor, my faith, determination, and the prayers of many supporters, you are smiling, knowing your story was told. Rest on, baby girl.

Mommy loves you.

A piece of my heart is in Heaven . . .

Sasha

1

It was Monday morning, and Sasha was at work, distraught and disoriented. It had to be a dream. As she paced around her desk, all she could think about was her best friend, Tina, and the incident at the restaurant on Saturday night. The awful confrontation between her and Tina took a toll on Sasha physically, mentally, and emotionally. She and Tina met in third grade and instantly became inseparable. They talked often and shared everything, from elementary school to adulthood.

Tina was Sasha's backbone through good and troubled times. She cried with Sasha when her father died in eighth grade. She was also there when Sasha's sister, Kellie, left for college, and Sasha felt deserted. Then, there was the time Tina was Sasha's moral support after her mother died, which was just after her high school graduation. At their mother's funeral, Sasha was still angry with Kellie and refused to acknowledge her.

Tina tried to be a mediator, but Sasha was too irrational. Kellie was devastated when she overheard Sasha say that Tina was her only sister. Kellie gazed at Tina and then back at Sasha and said, "Goodbye," then slipped away with hot tears rolling down her cheeks. Kellie didn't bother to look back. Sasha was also hurt because she didn't mean for Kellie to hear those mean words.

Sasha shuttered at the remembrance then flopped down in her desk chair, closed her eyes, and wept. She reflected on all the people she loved and lost through the years. She could not lose Tina, the one person who helped her weather the storms in her life. *How, when, and why did this happen?* she wondered.

Sasha jumped up. She needed to think. Were there signs or parts of conversations that she had overlooked?

There was an unbroken bond between the two friends, or so they thought. Sasha nearly made a path in the carpet. She hadn't been able to function since Saturday night. She felt dizzy. She desperately needed to figure out how to correct this wrong. The confrontation continued to replay over and over in her mind, even when she slept. Sasha was determined to find out how and why she and Tina ended up in such an ugly situation.

Sasha McMillan was a single, petite, but brick house of a woman. She was five-foot-eight inches tall, light brown-skinned, and had long thick black hair. Sasha was a beautiful Black woman and the chief executive officer of Sash Accounting Agency. She worked extremely hard for her accomplishments and invested long hours to get her business off the ground. After four years of challenging work on her own, she managed to build her company to where she needed to hire five loyal and dependable staff members. Hiring the staff was the best decision Sasha could have made, but after a while, she became grumpy. Many mornings she walked into the office with a frown. There was a time when the staff greeted her as she walked in. They said, "Good morning, Ms. Sasha."

"Morning," she replied without looking back. She abruptly stopped, turned over her shoulder, and then asked Betty, her first accountant, for a cup of coffee.

Sasha walked into her office and slammed the door without even realizing it.

"Right away," Betty responded under her breath. She felt dejected by Sasha's behavior.

Betty shared with her coworkers how Sasha had changed since she first started working at Sash Accounting Agency. Sasha used to be kindhearted and shared her weekend adventures with Betty every Monday morning. Betty was concerned about the drastic change in Sasha's attitude, so she got the group together and discussed a nice gift to get their boss for Christmas, which was only weeks away at that point.

Sasha gave wonderful gifts, specific for each of them, so they had no issues with pooling their money to buy her a gift she would appreciate. They bought two gift cards for Sasha. One to a day spa: Nalai at Park Hyatt in Midtown Manhattan and a six-month membership to the New York Sports Club in Midtown East. Both were twenty minutes from the office and thirty minutes from her condo. Sasha was excited about her gifts. She signed up for the gym in mid-January and went at least three times a week.

As Sasha paced in her office, distraught over the events of Saturday night, her thoughts took her back to the evening a tall, dark stranger took the treadmill next to her at the gym. He was handsome, but she did not say a word to him. He smiled at her as he set up the speed for his bike, but neither of them offered the first hello.

This continued for a week before the stranger gained the courage to speak to Sasha. She smiled, said hello, sped her treadmill, and then stared straight ahead. The next week, he strolled up to Sasha, just before she set up her treadmill, held out his hand, and began a conversation.

"Hi, I'm Glenn."

Sasha was thrilled he made the first move. She smiled and shook his hand.

"Nice to meet you, Glenn. I'm Sasha."

"Pretty name, Sasha. I thought I should introduce myself, given how we usually end up here around the same time."

"Yes, I noticed."

"So, are you busy after your workout? I'd like to offer you a cup of coffee or tea at the little shop downstairs, if you're up to it."

Sasha tried to hide her excitement. She had wished he would ask her out since the moment she first laid eyes on him. There was no way to mask the huge beam plastered on her face, so she nodded and then replied, "I'd like that."

After their workouts, they went downstairs to the coffee shop, sipped lattes, and chatted for hours. Glenn kept his eyes on this lovely lady. By their third coffee date, they exchanged telephone numbers.

Sasha almost tripped over the trash can in her office, bringing her back to reality. She halted and picked up the empty trash can. She shook her head, and her mind spun as fast as a Merry-go-Round.

"No! No!" she shouted.

She couldn't allow the memories of Glenn to infiltrate her thoughts while her relationship with Tina was doomed. How could she have allowed this to happen? Sasha grabbed her purse. She headed out of her office to get some fresh air. On her way out, she stumbled into Betty with a cup of coffee.

"Here, Sasha. I thought you might need another cup."

"Oh, Betty, I'm sorry. I need the rest of the day off. In fact, why don't all of you just take the rest of the day off?"

Betty was stunned. She stumbled over her words, trying to understand what was happening.

"Sasha! You ...you're scaring me. Is everything ok?"

"I just need a personal day, and I might as well give you all a holiday, too. Do me a favor and lock up everything."

Sasha got out of there before Betty or anyone else could ask more questions. She needed to clear her mind. She was out of breath and felt as though she just ran in a 5K race when she reached her car. She hopped in and sped away. The tires screeched, leaving the stench of the burning rubber.

She came to an abrupt stop in front of her condo. Before she knew it, she jumped out of her car, sprinted to the front door, unlocked it, then kicked it closed. As soon as the door slammed, Sasha's wails echoed throughout the home. She flung off her clothes as she ran into the bathroom. She stepped into the shower before the water could turn warm, and pressed the button on the CD player to "Nothing But Love" by Boney James.

Sasha closed her eyes as the chilly water ran down her body and the smooth jazz soothed her.

She must've been in there for twenty minutes or more. She felt better as she got out and dried herself off. She moseyed over to the dresser for a pair of pajamas, grabbed the remote control off the nightstand then pulled her comforter back before plopping onto the bed.

Though she had the remote in her hand, Sasha never turned on the TV. She immediately sank into her plush pillow and became deeply relaxed as she took long, soothing breaths into her nostrils, and then released them through her mouth. Ten minutes passed before she suddenly sat up in bed and looked around. It took a minute for her to focus, but she soon recognized her bedroom.

What? I'm home? she thought. Sasha was dazed and unsure if she was dreaming. She desperately tried to remember leaving work and driving home, let alone actually being in bed, draped in a pair of her favorite pajamas. Sasha sat on the side of the bed, far calmer than she'd been earlier, but still trying to understand why she was home. Then, it all came back. Her best friend of twenty-five years had been sleeping with the love of her life— Glenn.

The thought sent Sasha back into a whirlwind of emotions. She gently pulled her legs back into bed, threw the covers over her head, and cried until her soul felt empty.

Sasha

2

S asha wanted it to be a dream, but it wasn't. It was real. The altercation took place in Don Pepe's Restaurant on Saturday night. Though Sasha missed some relevant clues, she remembered Tina called her two months before to discuss her new man.

The morning of Tina's call, Sasha was still in bed. She slept in that Saturday morning after a long night out. When Sasha's cell rang, it startled her. She lunged at the phone, wondering who in the hell would call her so early.

She gazed at the clock on the wall and saw that it was actually 10:30 in the morning. She decided to pick up the phone and say hello.

"Hey, girl! What's up?" Tina was giddy because she had interesting news.

"Wow. You really can mess up a wet dream. I'm okay. How are you?"

Sasha and Tina hadn't been able to have their regular girl time due to Sasha's hectic schedule, so they only chatted for short moments at a time in the previous four months.

"Gurl," Tina almost sang. "You got to wake up. I need to tell you about my new man. Oh, and he is so fine!"

"Yeah, you're right. I need to sit up for this."

"Listen. Those other deadheads weren't about nothin'—with their black asses! But this one—his name is John. He is dark-skinned and sexy as hell. I had the royal fuck of my life! And you best believe he was the King."

Sasha laughed. "Wow. He must've been all that. I don't think I've ever heard you sound like this about anyone, Tina."

"He is amazing, Sasha. Girl, he took me out to dinner last night. After dinner, we went back to his place, and it was on, you hear me? It was ON!"

"How long have you been dating this guy?"

"Four months," Tina answered.

"Tina, be careful because I know how you have been hurt in past relationships."

"I'm not worried about this one. He is genuine and the real thing."

"Well, I'm really glad to hear that, sis. Listen. I'm beat. Let's chat a little later. I really need some sleep."

Tina promised Sasha she would catch up with her later if she was up to it. About two weeks later, she called Sasha back to see what she was doing. Tina invited her to dinner at Don Pepe to meet her new man.

Since Sasha didn't have plans for that Saturday, she agreed to meet Tina and her new man. So, it was a date. Tina was excited. She couldn't wait for Sasha to meet John.

Sasha suddenly realized she would be the third wheel, so she figured she better call someone to join her. She told Tina she would bring Glenn along. Sasha and Glenn had been serious for six months, and it was well past time for Tina to meet him anyway. Tina was delighted.

Sasha found herself without a date because Glenn had some unfinished business to handle. He asked her to pardon him this once because there was a matter he really needed to clear up. Sasha was a little bummed about going solo. She always felt that two is a couple and three is a crowd. She started to postpone until Glenn was available because she really didn't want to be a third wheel. However, she and Tina hadn't hung out in a while, and Sasha certainly wanted to meet this John fella, given all the good things Tina said about him.

Sasha decided that it would be in her best interest to call Michael, an ex-boyfriend, to be her date. This way, she wouldn't have to feel so out of place. She picked up her cell phone and dialed

Michael's number, hoping he wasn't with one of his patients. She was about to hang up when he answered on the fifth ring, sounding groggy.

"Good morning, Michael, this is Sasha. Did I wake you?"

"Hey, Sasha. No problem. I just finished a thirty-six-hour shift. I was tired and slept in late. What's up?"

"I was calling to see if you were available tonight, and if so, would you be willing to escort me to dinner? I need a date. I don't want to be a third wheel with my friend and her new man."

"What time do you want me to pick you up?"

"Be here at seven-thirty, and Michael, don't be late."

"Okay, okay! I'll be on time. So, who is this friend? Anybody I know?"

"Um, yeah. It's Tina."

Michael let out a loud huff. "You know I don't care for that girl."

"Yes, I know, but Tina's cool. You just don't understand her like I do. Michael, please don't back out on me now."

"Sasha, I will go to the moon with you."

"Even if Tina is on it?"

He huffed again, and then reluctantly said, "Yeah—even if Tina is on it."

"Thanks, Michael. Can't wait to see you."

Sasha hung up the phone, smiled, and thought about how reliable Michael is.

That evening seemed to have come extremely fast for Sasha. She was excited to finally see Tina again and also meet her new man. When she and Michael arrived at the restaurant, Sasha spotted Tina, but there was no one at the table with her. She and Michael walked over and sat down.

"Hey, Tina. I hope you don't mind, but I had to bring Michael along. Glenn is busy tonight."

"Oh, that's cool. Hey, Michael. Longtime, no see." Tina smirked knowing she irritated him.

"Hey, Tina. How are you?" Michael said, struggling to offer kind words.

"I'm great. Thanks for asking."

Sasha reached for a piece of bread in the basket and then asked Tina where her mystery man was. She glanced around the restaurant, wondering where he could be.

"He's in the men's room." Tina glanced in the direction of the restrooms. "He should be back any minute."

The waiter came to take their orders. Tina asked if he would give them a couple of minutes, so he nodded and left. She peeked toward the men's room again and saw John on his way out.

"Oh, here comes John now," she said.

Sasha's back was turned, so she couldn't see him as he approached. When the tall, dark, and handsome gentleman sat down and spoke, Sasha's mouth fell open. She recognized him immediately. Her eyes nearly popped out of her head.

"Glenn," Sasha announced more so than asked. "What are you doing here?"

"Sasha. Why are you here?" he responded.

Tina's chair fell backward as she jumped out of her seat.

"What the HELL is going on here? Sasha, how do you know my man?"

Sasha glared at Glenn and then turned back to Tina. "Is this your mystery man? Your *king*?"

Tina replied, matter-of-factly. "Yes, and I need to know what the hell is going on here?"

Sasha glared at Tina. "I'm just as confused as you are." She turned her attention to Glenn. "What's really going on, Glenn? You had some business to tend to, huh?"

Michael sat speechless, glancing back and forth between the three of them.

Sasha noticed Glenn's complexion was flushed. He responded in a low tone.

"Boo, this was the situation I told you I needed to clear up."

"Boo, hell!" Tina leaned forward and slammed her fist on the table. "Sasha, are you sleeping with my man?" Tina exploded. Her nostrils flared as she breathed loudly and sweated profusely.

"Your man? I never knew he was *your* man."

Sasha shook her head in disbelief. She and Glenn had been dating for six months. How did Glenn get to be Tina's man? Glenn—John—the man both women loved was in as much disbelief as they were. He sat with his mouth open as the two of them tried to sort things out.

"Tina, I told you Glenn and I have been seeing each other for six months." You never said you knew him."

"Six months shit," Tina replied. "I've been with him four months, and what the hell?" Tina turned to Glenn. "Glenn? *Glenn?*" she repeated. "I thought your name was John."

John barked at Tina. "Wait, doggone it!" A hush came over the entire area as patrons seemed to notice tempers flaring. "First, I am *not* your man. We already had that conversation. We were NEVER a couple."

Sasha glanced up and peered into Tina's eyes as they looked weary. Though Tina was motionless, Sasha could see hurt, pain, and coldness oozing from her friend. Sasha knew what she saw, she would never forget. The whole situation with Tina made her feel helpless, and she was unsure of how to mend their friendship or their broken hearts after this. Sasha's feet were cemented to the floor as tears rolled down her cheeks.

Tina ran out before Sasha could do or say anything to stop her. Sasha wanted to ask Glenn more questions, but her mind was in shambles. She didn't even realize tears flooded her face. Glenn reached for her hand.

"Sasha, I'll take you home," he said.

Michael quickly jumped up. "Hold on, partner. She came with me. I brought her here, so I'll be the one to take her home. The best thing for you to do is run after your girlfriend."

Glenn relented as Michael wrapped his arm around Sasha and led her out of the restaurant. He remained at the table alone. He couldn't believe Sasha and Tina were best friends. Oh, and what the hell? Why was Sasha there with another man? The pain in his chest left him winded and weak. He finally got himself together and left twenty minutes later.

Tina

3

T ina sat at her kitchen table with her third cup of coffee. The caffeine was what kept her moving. Her nerves were all over the place. She couldn't eat anything. Food was her enemy as she gagged even when she tried to take a bite of toast. She hadn't been able to eat since Saturday morning. All her strength and energy were spent crying.

Tina couldn't wrap her mind around the fact that her best friend and her man had sex. She remembered grabbing her purse and leaving the restaurant. Once outside, she realized she didn't have a way home. Her sister had given her a ride to the restaurant. She refused to go back inside, so she stomped down the street, about a block away before she flagged a cab.

Like Sasha, Tina Miller was also petite, five-foot-five with junk in her trunk. Her skin tone was dark chocolate that glowed. Tina wore her hair in a short afro that framed her beautiful face just right. She was wild, outspoken, and fun to be with. Although she was small in size, Tina could always manage her own. Sasha admired her spunkiness. After they graduated from high school, Tina wanted to take a break from school. She later decided to attend Passaic County Community College. She graduated with an associate degree in science. Her goal was to become a lawyer and own a home by the age of thirty-five. At this point, she still had a few years to go before she would achieve that goal. She set goals for herself and worked as a personal attendant for an elderly woman by day and as a part-time cashier at J.C. Penney in the evening.

Tina applied for a six-month, paralegal certificate at Kaplan University in her hometown of Passaic, New Jersey. After four months into the program, she accepted a paid internship at Brown and Brown Law Firm in New York. She quit her job in order to continue the internship and took public transportation to New York until she graduated. Brown and Brown Law Firm is where she met Attorney John G. Saunders. His office was on the third floor.

Tina worked on the second floor for Attorney Larry C. Brown. He was tall, had a dark complexion, a salt-and-pepper beard, and a baritone voice. Everyone called the boss L.C. He often collaborated with John, or J. as he liked to call him, and his group of lawyers. Tina took her work seriously and was an excellent paralegal. Three weeks into her internship, L.C. encouraged her to work two days a week upstairs with the Saunders Firm. He felt she would be an asset to the team, and it also would be a beneficial learning experience. L.C. introduced Tina to the third-floor staff, but only three attorneys were present that day.

Tina ended up spending twenty-five percent of her time, twice a week, as an assistant at the Saunders Firm. It was two weeks before she met Mr. Saunders.

One morning, Tina entered the lobby of the third floor, and a six-foot-tall, Denzell Washington, look-alike stared her way. The folders she had in her hands fell to the floor. Her eyes bulged, her hands were sweaty, and butterflies fluttered in her stomach as he walked towards her with his hand stretched. He bent down to help her pick up the folders.

"Hello, Tina." He knew this stranger had to be the new girl L.C. told him about. "I'm John G. Saunders," he continued. "I've heard wonderful things about your work."

John never told anyone in the office what his middle initial meant. Though Tina heard his introduction, she couldn't process it. She was frozen in her tracks.

Gloria the secretary spoke up and said, "Tina, this is our boss."

Tina's trance was broken. She felt foolish, but she slid her wet hand into his and shook it.

"Glad to meet you, Mr. Saunders."

"In this office, we address each other by first names–unless, of course, if we're with clients or in a conference, then we should keep it professional with Mr. and Ms."

He let go of her hand and strolled into his office. Gloria broke out in laughter as soon as he closed his office door.

"Girl, close your mouth." Gloria was amused.

Tina walked over and asked where he had been hiding. She knew the other three lawyers were married, so her radar was buzzing for information about this man. Gloria explained that he was not married, didn't date employees, interns or office helpers, he owned a townhouse in upstate New York and a house somewhere in Jersey. Tina hadn't heard anything Gloria said beyond, "He wasn't married."

Tina went to work early the rest of the week to stake out what time John arrived. She also made note of what time he left work. Once she had his schedule down, she stepped on the elevator behind him the following Monday. She prayed the elevator would fill up so she could move closer to him, and it did. She eased so close to him that her arm pressed against his. She silently hoped he noticed her new outfit and smelled her expensive perfume.

When he got off the elevator without so much as offering a compliment, Tina knew she would go harder. She would ensure that Mr. Saunders would be her man by any means necessary, and he would be glad about it.

Tina

4

T ina's head was spinning. She tapped her feet and felt jittery. She jumped from the kitchen table, went to the living room, and looked out of the window. She was cold. She began to shiver, and her teeth chattered, but she soon mellowed out as the heat from the sun on the glass window warmed her. She turned around and ran into her bedroom, flopping face-first onto her bed. Soon, Tina fell asleep.

When Tina woke up, she had no idea how long she had been asleep. She pulled herself up slowly on the bed and sat on the edge. She decided to go into the kitchen and make herself a ham and cheese sandwich and pulled out a Pepsi to wash it down. She took her snack back into the bedroom, sat in the chair next to the bed, and turned on the television. An hour later, Tina felt better and walked over to her closet to choose an outfit for work.

When she opened the door to the closet, she stood, staring at her new wardrobe. It was then that Tina remembered her second attempt at catching John's eye.

Since John hadn't given Tina the attention she wanted the week she met him, she knew it was time to step up her game, so she went shopping the following weekend.

When Monday came again, Tina was front and center, ready to squeeze behind the group of men as they entered the elevator. She paused in front of the open doors as the men made room for her. This time, she noticed all eyes were on her, including John's. She wore a yellow dress that accentuated her body in all the right places. She eased into the elevator, filling it not only with her bold presence but also with her sensuous aroma. John and the others complimented her. Even L.C. told her how nice she looked, but Tina only heard John's compliment. She felt heat radiate throughout her body.

However, the next morning, to Tina's dismay, John wasn't at the elevator. She wondered if he was running late, or if he'd gotten there early. She got off on the second floor and trudged into her office. Around 12:00 P.M., she noticed that L.C. wasn't in his office, so she asked Ruthie, his secretary, if he was okay.

Like Tina, Ruthie was in her thirties, beautiful, and just a few inches shorter than Tina. While Tina was on the slimmer side, Ruthie's voluptuous body had enough curves for them both. Ruthie loved her Hispanic roots and brought plantains in her signature Puerto Rican dishes for lunch nearly every day. She wore wigs, and she wore a different one every week. Tina liked Ruthie because she was a party girl, and Tina could pump her for information.

Ruthie told her that L.C. and John had to be in Boston to close on a big case. Tina wondered why she was left out of the loop. She nodded and then told Ruthie she'd be back.

Tina took the elevator to the third floor and was immediately met by Gloria with an office rumor. John went on a date over the weekend. Tina's heart dropped at the news. She didn't address Gloria. She just turned and walked back to the elevator.

Gloria was in her early forties though she didn't appear to be older than thirty. Her skin was silky-brown, and she always seemed to glow. She kept her hair and body tight. Unlike Ruthie, Tina couldn't pump Gloria for information that wasn't associated with work.

On her way home, Tina fantasized about being with John in an intimate setting. She had a rival but was determined to get John for herself.

She thought she had to up her game once again, and this time, may the best woman win.

The following morning, Tina was met at her office by lots of commotion. Everyone was loud, but they all had smiles. She rushed to find out what was happening. Ruthie informed her of the case John and L.C. won. There would be a big celebration Thursday night because John would be busy on a date that Friday.

Hearing John had a date Friday didn't faze Tina. She smiled because this was her chance to make her move, and she had two days to devise her plan. Ruthie and Tina decided they would travel to the party together. Tina made plans to get dressed at Ruthie's place before the shindig.

The night before the party, Tina grabbed a glass and a bottle of wine from the fridge and then went to her closet to piece together an outfit that would surely make John's eyes undress her. She chose a pair of skin-tight, dark-blue denim jeans and a blue camisole. She also matched her outfit with a pair of blue denim stilettos and a denim jacket. Tina sang and danced as she packed her outfit in an overnight bag.

The next morning, Tina was off to work with her overnight bag in tow. Thankfully, the workday came and went quickly. Ruthie was glad to have Tina over to her place before the party. She was glad to finally have someone in the office she could hang with.

Though the party started at 7:00, the women left Ruthie's townhouse in enough time to be fashionably late. Tina decided they should each drive their own cars in case the other wanted to leave early. She sat in her car, tidying her makeup when Ruthie tapped on her window. She let the window down.

"Hey, are you coming or what?" Ruthie asked.

"Yeah. I just need a minute. You go ahead. I'll be in shortly."

Ruthie left Tina, primping. Tina sat in the car until 8:00 P.M., then sashayed into Dave and Buster's with all eyes on her.

Ruthie spotted Tina and then signaled for her to come over. The attorneys' wives' eyes all widen at the sight of Tina as she sashayed in the place. They wondered who this beautiful woman was whose clothes looked as if they had been painted on her. Once at their table, Ruthie introduced her to everyone. Tina nodded and then glanced around the place. She didn't recognize anyone from the office.

"Ruthie, where's everyone?" Tina asked.

"L.C. and John are at the bar, getting drinks," Ruthie answered.

Tina pivoted towards the bar without another word. John and L.C. spotted her at the same time.

"What a woman. She looks astonishing," L.C. complimented as Tina made her way to them.

Tina propped herself on a stool between the two men and then winked at John. With her back to L.C., he picked up his drink and then gave John a see-ya-later look along with a two-finger salute off his forehead before walking away.

The bartender placed a drink and a napkin in front of John. He held his hand up for the bartender to wait then turned to Tina.

"Would you like something to drink?" John asked.

"Sure. Your Long Island Iced Tea will do," Tina replied, reaching for his drink.

He picked it up before she could. "Whoa. I think you need to know I asked for a double shot of vodka in this."

"And?"

"You sure you can manage it?"

Tina looked at him, took the drink out of his hand, and then hopped off the stool.

"Just so you know: I've mastered handling stronger things." She turned and walked away.

John watched her prance back to the area of the party. She sat at the end of the bench and left enough room for him to sit next to her. The others in the group had ordered their food by the time John returned to the table.

Once everyone finished eating, they got up to play games–all with the exception of Tina, John, and Ruthie. Ruthie downed the last of her drink and then decided she wanted to play the games as well.

"Tina, let's go and play the machines."

Tina winked at Ruthie. "Go ahead. I'll meet up with you after I visit the restroom."

Ruthie smiled and walked off. In bold, Tina-like fashion, she slid closer to John.

"Why is a handsome man like you all alone?"

"I could ask why you're alone as well."

"I'm not. You're here next to me."

"My lady had previous obligations tonight. She would've been here." John repositioned himself on the seat, creating a little more space between them.

"So, you're in a committed relationship?"

"It's new, but it certainly looks promising."

Tina had heard enough for now. She stood and left to find Ruthie. She was ready to leave.

Once home, Tina was in a bit of a rage. She flung a glass of wine across the kitchen and banged her fist against the wall. She was angry with herself, wondering how in the hell she let that dick get away. She was hard on herself for not being more assertive.

She walked into her bedroom. She looked toward her bed and imagined John as he lay naked there. She went to the drawer for her new vibrator.

As she stared at the skin tone, she imagined it was John's penis.

Tina walked over to the bed and threw the covers back, crawled into the middle of the bed, and positioned herself to take John's stiff penis in her wet vagina. She screamed, tossed, and turned until she fell asleep with John's penis in her hand.

Tina woke up the next morning with the toy still in her hand. She smiled, jumped out of bed, and went into the bathroom to prepare for work.

She dressed up in a skinned-tight dark green jumpsuit and gold sandals that she took out of the closet the previous night. Before Tina left for work, she took a final look in the mirror at herself and was pleased with how she looked. She was adamant to have a closer relationship with John.

Tina drove around the parking lot once she arrived at work. She was looking for John's car and realized he wasn't there yet. So, she sat in her car until she saw him walking into the building. Tina jumped out of her car and fell in steps behind John as he entered the elevator. She blushed and her lips turned into a smile when he bid her good morning.

Tina stepped out of the elevator on her floor turned and waved at John before the door closed. As she walked into the office, Ruthie rushed over to Tina.

"L.C. called an emergency meeting and needs you to answer the incoming calls."

"What? I'll go upstairs and work with Gloria."

"No! You have to work here. This is a joint meeting."

John walked in with his staff. He looked straight ahead as he passed Ruthie and spoke. L.C. called Ruthie into the conference room and closed the door. Tina was furious for being left out, and John didn't acknowledge her at that time.

Tina turned around and walked over to her cubicle. She slumped down in a chair in front of her computer and signed on to a dating site. Tina refused to let go of the idea that she and John weren't a couple. She tried to find a match to go on a date to use as a pun to make John jealous. She searched until the meeting was over to no avail.

Sasha

5

Although fall was only weeks away, it felt like fall already. Sasha stood on her terrace with her arms wrapped across her chest. There was a briskness in the air, the sun was out. She hadn't been to the gym or anywhere for a while. So, she decided to go running in the park near her condo.

Sasha rushed inside, ran into her bedroom, and chose a red jogging suit and red sneakers. Once she was dressed, she did one last check before she would leave for the park. When she saw herself in the mirror, dressed in all red, she remembered her first date with Glenn. He called her two weeks after they met at the gym. He wanted to take her to dinner and a movie.

She was so excited that she left work early to go home and get ready. On the way home, she thought about the undergarments she was going to wear and what color. She knew that red was Glenn's favorite color, so she went to Victoria's Secret to buy something sexy. While in the store, she stopped to think. She wondered if Glenn was really going to see what was under her clothes.

Sasha checked the price tags on the pieces in her hands. *If I spend fifty-two dollars for a bra and a pair of thongs, he better snatch my clothes OFF!* She laughed aloud at herself. Once at her apartment, she went directly to soak in a hot bubble bath with aromatic candles around the tub. She turned on her favorite jazz before climbing into the tub to relax and think about how the night would possibly end.

After her relaxing bath, Sasha went to the closet and pulled out a red mini-dress with a low-cut back. The dress was a precise fit, exposing that baby got back. She stood in the mirror and spritzed on Dream Angels Heavenly by Victoria's Secret, thinking of how Glenn would enjoy watching her move around the restaurant floor. When the doorbell rang, it was Glenn with a dozen yellow roses.

"Are you ready?" he asked.

"Yes, but are you ready for me?" Sasha smiled.

They both laughed. She placed the roses in a vase and set the vase on the kitchen counter. Once outside, Glenn opened the car door for her, and off they went. He took her to Jezebel, one of the best restaurants in town, and ordered a bottle of Dom

Pérignon. Sasha enjoyed every moment with Glenn. After the movie, he took Sasha back to her condo. She offered him to come in for a while.

"Yes," he replied quickly.

Sasha and Glenn sat and talked until 3:00 A.M., and then Glenn realized how late it was.

"I guess I will be leaving, Sasha. It's pretty late."

Sasha was upset because she was ready to take him to bed. Just looking at him made her horny. She kept her composure and released a soft sigh.

"Okay. Let me walk you to the door."

Glenn stopped at the door then turned and gave her a sweet, slow kiss. In an instant, Sasha was wet all over, and her red thongs begin to stick to her. She closed the door behind him, and then she went to take a cold shower before bed.

As Sasha reminisced on her first date with Glenn, tears streamed down her cheeks. When she looked in the mirror, she was uncomfortable with what she saw. She was extremely sad and decided she had to get out of the house to clear her mind of those memories.

Sasha walked the block to the park, warmed up, and ran for over an hour, trying to forget about Glenn. But she couldn't stop thinking about him. Sasha was reminded of Glenn wherever she looked. There were couples of all ages, walking, talking, smiling, and holding hands. She couldn't tolerate the pain she felt any longer, so she turned around and ran back in the direction of her condo.

Once inside, she flopped on the sofa and cried herself to sleep. It was past noon when Sasha woke up. She still had Glenn on her mind, but she was also starving. As she went into the kitchen, Sasha remembered a psychological fact: being unable to get someone off your mind, could very well mean that you are also on that person's mind. She wondered if Glenn longed for her as much as she did him.

Sasha looked into the fridge, but there were only cold cuts and no bread. She had to decide whether to go grocery shopping or go to a restaurant. Reluctantly, Sasha decided to go to Olive Garden for an early dinner. As she walked into the restaurant, she had second thoughts about her decision to dine alone but she stayed anyway.

A hostess came and led her to a booth. Once seated, her waitress handed her a menu, and then she ordered a drink. There was a group of women sitting in the booth on the opposite side of Sasha. It appeared they were celebrating something. The more they drank the louder they became. One of the older women noticed Sasha dining alone and decided to invite her to join them.

She walked over to Sasha's booth and said, "Hello, I'm sorry to bother you, but my name is Jane."

"Hello, Jane. It's no bother. I'm Sasha."

"I noticed you're sitting alone and was wondering if you would like to join us at our booth. We're here to celebrate with my niece. She got engaged last night."

"Oh, how wonderful, Jane, and so sweet of you to offer me to join you. Thank you, but I'm waiting for my friend who will be here any minute."

"Ok, Sasha. Just thought I would offer. Enjoy your meal."

Sasha felt jabbed in her stomach when she heard the word engaged. Suddenly, she wasn't hungry anymore. Sasha ordered a meal and then asked the waitress to pack her food to go. She had to get away as fast as she could. When she heard the word engaged, she thought of the night Glenn proposed to her.

On her drive home, she remembered that incredibly special night. That morning, Glenn called Sasha to ask her to dinner. Little did she know, he had something special to discuss with her. She insisted on making him a home-cooked meal, so Glenn agreed.

Later that night, Sasha got ready for her man. She made dinner—steak, baked potatoes, and salad with red wine on the side. Glenn arrived on time. He was there at exactly 7:30 P.M.

"Mmm…something smells good," he said once he stepped inside. Sasha slayed over the stove for him—something she seldomly did since she lived alone and worked many hours. Glenn just smiled when he noticed her beautiful dress.

"I take it you're ready to eat, so I will fix our plates while you get comfortable." Sasha headed toward the kitchen.

"Thanks, babe."

Glenn went over to have a seat on the sofa. Sasha's place was dimly lit with three-wick candles and soft music. Sasha prepared the plates quickly and called him over to the table. As she set the plates, Glenn poured their wine.

They chatted over dinner, and then Sasha picked up her empty glass, ready to pour more wine. That's when she noticed something inside the glass. It was a diamond ring. She looked at Glenn with excitement and tears in her eyes.

"Glenn! What is this?"

He beamed inside. "What does it look like?

Glenn slid back his chair and dropped to one knee.

"Babe," he said, staring up at Sasha. "I know we've only been together for six months, but you mean more to me than I can ever express. All I know is I love you, and I want my forever to include you. Sasha McMillan, will you marry me?"

Sasha couldn't stop crying if she wanted to. Glenn meant the world to her also. She hadn't imagined this day would come so soon. She managed to answer through gobs of tears.

"Yes, yes, yes," she said. "Without a doubt. I will marry you, Glenn."

The drive home from Olive Garden's seemed to go by quickly as Sasha relished the memory of her engagement day. When she pulled up in front of her condo, the front of her shirt was saturated with tears. She went inside, plopped on her sofa, and wondered how or what could she do to mend her broken heart.

She wallowed in her sorrow for a few minutes then slowly got off the sofa, inched her way over to the phone, and fumbled as she dialed Glenn's number. Sasha hesitated. In fact, she never said a word once he answered. Her legs turned to jelly. She slid down onto the floor in a fetal position, and softly moaned as Glenn called her name and begged her to talk to him.

Tina

6

As Tina continued to fan through her wardrobe, she did so with little cognizance of what she was doing. Her thoughts were still of the time when she decided to peruse an online dating site.

After weeks on the site and going on one date, Tina was disappointed with the guy and gave up on the site. She was in pursuit of John despite how many times he rejected her advances. Tina thought all she needed to do next was be in the right place at the right time. So, she followed John for days without him knowing it. She discovered he was consistent about going to the gym a few nights a week, so she conveniently showed up there with a plan to get some alone time with him.

John was in awe when he saw Tina step on the treadmill next to him. He was in full trot, so he only acknowledged her with a wave. After a half hour, on cue, Tina received the call she expected from her mother. She slowed the treadmill then answered her phone, pretending to be surprised.

"Hi, Mom," she answered. She paused as her mother spoke, and then continued. "Dinner? Sure. I'll be there."

Tina had persuaded her mother to prepare a special dinner, stating she would be bringing her new boyfriend to meet the family. Tina stepped off the treadmill and moved away from John. She lowered her voice so he couldn't hear her conversation. After hanging up with her mother, she strolled over to John's treadmill. He was in the middle of his cooling-down phase, walking at a moderate pace.

"Hey, that was my mother. She cooked a hefty meal and asked if I would like to come over. Are you hungry?"

"I will get something from the café downstairs before I leave," he said through panted breaths.

"My mother is an excellent cook, and she always makes plenty, so you're welcome to come as my guest."

John hesitated and was a bit confused why Tina would invite him to her family's dinner. "Well, I am hungry, but I don't think it would be appropriate for me to show up at your family's dinner."

"Oh, my parents are used to me bringing guests, but suit yourself. I just thought you might be hungry and would enjoy some good company."

As Tina gathered her things, John suddenly thought a home-cooked meal would be great.

Upon their arrival, Tina led John to the den, where her father sat, watching TV. She asked him to wait for her while she helped her mother and sister in the kitchen. Tina was back only moments later and handed John a glass of cognac.

Ten minutes later, she stepped into the den to let the men know dinner was ready.

John snatched his glass and followed Tina into the dining room. Dinner was delicious, and the conversation was mostly about how Tina and John knew each other as well as their careers. After dinner, the men retreated to the den while the women took the dishes into the kitchen.

By the time Tina finished in the kitchen, she walked into the living room and found both John and her father asleep. She walked over and tapped John on the shoulder. He was in a daze. He tried to stand up but slumped back into the chair. Tina turned sideways and looked at the cognac bottle. She realized her father and John had finished the bottle. John was too intoxicated to get home on his own.

She smiled. This was her opportunity to get what she wanted. She asked John for his keys and insisted she drive him home, stating her sister would pick her up from his place.

John rambled the address to his townhouse in New York and the code needed to enter the gate. She drove into the garage, parked the car, and hurried to help him out of the car. He leaned on her shoulder as he pressed the code into the electronic keypad, and they walked inside. She watched as John bolted down a hallway that she assumed led to his bedroom.

Tina walked into the living room. It was stunning—a white leather sofa and loveseat in the center of the huge room with black-and-white pillows and white curtains at the double windows that overlooked the Hudson River.

John slipped into the living room and found Tina sitting quietly looking down at her phone.

"Where's your ride, Tina?"

"She's not answering my calls. I left several messages for her.

John immediately retreated into his master bedroom and returned with linens and pillows for her.

"Lay down and rest, until your sister gets here, and wake me so I can lock up behind you."

"Okay, thank you."

Tina was excited to be in his townhouse, and despite his drunken state, he was being so attentive to her. Her plan had worked so far. All she had to do at this point was to time everything correctly.

Tina slipped out of her dress and draped it over the back of the loveseat. She sat on the sofa, slipped out of her stilettos, and lay on the sofa. Her plan was to wait until John was asleep, then slip into his bedroom and slide in bed naked with him. When she heard him snoring, she put her plan into action. She stepped into the bedroom. The silhouette of his strong body with the broadest shoulders she had ever seen set her on cum-ready.

Tina's eyes traveled down to his six-pack, the lower her eyes went, the more excited she got. She stopped, and her eyes widen at his stiff penis. She tiptoed closer to the bed. She eased down as close as she could and pressed her naked body against his.

John stirred from the warmth of her body next to his. Tina took this as approval. She took her middle finger, slid it down the center of his chest, and stopped at his penis. She wrapped her hand around it and held it.

She had an urgency to feel it inside of her. She threw her leg across his body, slid her vagina down on his penis, and began to ride it. His body responded to her actions, and before he knew it, he began thrusting into her mound of heat. Tina's loud moans turned him on even more. He hoped his walls were insulated because she seemed to get louder with every thrust.

Tina shook uncontrollably as they each reached their peak. She eased off of John's body while he lay limp for a moment. A few minutes later, he managed to gather himself and then rushed out of bed and into the bathroom.

Tina was disappointed when John suddenly hopped out of bed without a word. She expected a different outcome and felt rejected by his behavior. When she heard the shower, she could only imagine what went on in John's mind.

Tina went into the living room and snatched up her cell phone before heading into the guest bathroom. Once she stepped out of the bathroom, she noticed John sitting solemnly. He was on the sofa looking at his hands. He turned towards her. The looked she saw in his eyes concerned her, but she refused to let it put a damper on how she felt.

"Hey, my sister is on her way."

John dropped his head and then nodded. He didn't bother to look up again. They sat in silence until her sister arrived. John walked Tina out, only offering a quick wave of goodbye.

Tina's mind was filled with thoughts of her sexual escapade with John. It had been the most enjoyable fuck she ever had and would not be the last one. In her mind, John was her man after what she put on him. She would never let him forget that night or let him go without a fight. On her ride home, all she could think about was how she would get back in his bed. She couldn't wait to see him the next morning.

John

7

J ohn was mystified and angry with himself for not having enough balls to tell Sasha about what happened with Tina. He never imagined she and Tina even knew each other. He found himself pacing inside the living room of his condo, trying to figure out the pieces of his life. He was engaged to Sasha, and he loved her very much. John wondered if Sasha would ever forgive him, or even trust him again. If only he had told her about what happened with him and the intern at his office, he might have saved both, Sasha and him, some heartache. He had botched his relationship for a dinner and fuck with Tina, and now, after that Saturday at Don Pepe's, Sasha had the wrong idea about everything.

John rocked his head in disbelief. How and why did he let his guard down to trust Tina? He knew she was a conniving bitch. Yet, he fell prey to her plot. John went over to the window and began to daydream. His mind was flooded with thoughts of the night he slept with Tina. The night he dreaded was still truly clear—almost as if it was yesterday.

John trudged back into his apartment after walking Tina out that night. He was furious about what happened between him and Tina. His knees buckled, he flopped on the sofa, dropped his head into his hand, and fussed. It seemed like a dream, mostly like a nightmare. He never planned for this to happen.

Tina was beautiful, intelligent, and a flirtatious woman. He tried hard to keep a business-friendly relationship with her. John was in a relationship with the incredibly beautiful Sasha McMillan, and he managed to develop serious feelings for her. What would she think of him and this unfortunate incident?

The morning after, John leaped from his sofa and grabbed his phone to call the office. He spoke with Gloria. He told her he would be out of the office for a couple of days, and not to give anyone and he meant no one, any information about him or his absences. He hung up the phone with Gloria and called the one person he needed to speak with—his dad.

"Hello, son," his dad answered. "It's always good to hear from you, but what's happening? I wasn't expecting a call this early."

"I'm okay, Dad. I need to speak with you in person though."

"Son, are you sure you're okay?"

"Dad, I will discuss it with you once I arrive. I should be there within an hour."

John's dad was his and his brothers' advisor. They could talk to him about every and anything. He would be attentive, while his sons talked, and he would give them his perception of the situation. He knew when things were serious, and what he heard in John's voice was panic.

The drive usually took John fifteen minutes, but this time, the ride was longer. He took his time because he needed to gather his thoughts on how to share the news with his dad. John parked and leaped out of his car, jogged up the stairs to the front door, and there stood his dad, John Henry. John Henry grabbed him by his hand and pulled him into his arms. After breaking their embrace, they went into the den. There was a small table nearby with any and everything imaginable to eat or drink plus the chess board.

"Son, what's wrong? You sound like it was an emergency."

"Dad, what is this setup for?" John pointed to the table of food and drinks.

"I thought we might need treats to energize us. You implied this was an urgent situation, and it might take time to resolve the issues."

His father reached for a Danish and a bottle of juice.

"Dad, I just need to talk, and for you to listen."

"Okay, Son. I will eat and listen while you talk." He bit into the Danish. "You better have some."

"That's ok, Dad."

John described the situation with Tina and what went down at his townhouse the night before. He felt terrible because he didn't like her in that way and didn't know how this would influence them on the job.

"Who the heck is Tina? Your mom and I thought you were with that nice girl named Sasha. Son, what happened to Sasha?"

"Dad please—"

"Okay, Son, you got your old man's attention. What happened?"

"Dad, Tina drove me home, and I invited her in to wait for her sister."

"Hold on, Son. Let me get a shot of cognac. I have a feeling this is going to be good."

"I fell asleep. When I woke up, she was riding my penis like a wild woman, and I'm sure her loud moaning and groaning could be heard blocks away."

"Son, did you enjoy it?"

"Dad, be serious."

"Son, I am as serious as a heart attack." His dad laughed.

"Well, just say I am not responsible for what happened. I was ashamed, felt dirty, used, and had a panic attack afterward."

"Son, are you upset because Tina started the sexual act instead of you?"

"No! I'm upset because she knew I have a woman, and now, she's placed me in a predicament. Do I tell Sasha? And what about work? Do I continue letting Tina assist in my office?"

"Son, what does your heart say to do? Would telling Sasha hurt her?"

"I'm sure it would, Dad, and I can't do that. I'm ready to propose to Sasha. I love her."

His dad jumped up, knocking over the table with a loud crash.

"Congratulations, Son." There was a knock. His dad glanced at the door to the den. "That's your nosy mother. I wonder how long she was there, listening. Come in, Eva," he said.

Eva entered the room, smiling. "Glenn, come and give your mother a hug. What are you two doing behind closed doors?"

He stood to give his mother—his first love—a warm embrace.

"Eva, our son is going to propose to Sasha."

"What? Oh my, Glenn! When are you going to propose?"

"Soon, Mom."

"Good," John Henry said. "Listen. Call that woman, Tina, and set a date to sit down and talk to her about what happened. Oh, and use some of your strong yet delicate words I hear you saying in the courtroom sometimes."

"Right, Dad."

"What's this about, John Henry?" Eva interjected.

"Nothing, Eva. I'm talking to my son."

"Well, he's my son, too."

John interjected. "I'll let you both know when I need help planning the engagement dinner."

John said his goodbyes and headed home. He decided he would call Tina later to set up a time and place to meet with her. He needed to let her know what happened could not or would not happen again. John exhaled all his negative feelings and decided to surprise Sasha with dinner later.

He stepped inside his townhouse. The fragrance of gardenia greeted him. He noticed his housekeeper had changed his linens, remade his bed, cleaned both bathrooms, hung clean towels, and vacuumed the carpets. She did a terrific job of cleaning up the earlier nightmare. John plopped down on the sofa, hit the button on the radio, and fell asleep listening to easy jazz. He jumped off the sofa, and then checked his watch for the time. He had two hours to get dressed and pick up Sasha to make their seven o'clock reservation at Sea Shack in Hoboken, New Jersey.

John enjoyed his dinner with Sasha and decided not to allow the tryst with Tina to creep into his mind. After dinner with the love of his life, he bid her goodnight, and then went home. He parked his car and went inside his townhouse with a smile on his face.

After briefly dozing on the sofa, John bounced up quickly. He had taken two days off work and needed to make sure he was up with everything before he went back to face Tina.

John's legs were cement as he shuffled his heavy feet across the carpet. He slowly approached the picture window once again. The sky was dark compared to the blue sky that morning. He shook his head repeatedly. He tried to get the picture of the darkness that represented Tina's evil spirit and her conniving attributes out of his mind.

John turned slowly and went into his home office to do some work. But his mind wasn't on work. He was so confused. He scratched his head wondering how in the hell did Tina persuade her family to be a part of her scheme or were they aware of her plot? John decided it would be best if he got some rest, so he went to bed.

John

8

That morning, John woke up early. He hadn't done much work the night before. So, he jumped out of bed, rushed into the bathroom, took a shower, and got dressed. He grabbed a cup of coffee before he went into his home office. John and L.C. partnered again to work on a high-profile criminal trial. He checked his notes for errors before the conference with L.C. during the week. After an hour, he felt confident that he was updated, and he left for work.

John dreaded going back after having some time away from the office. Just as he expected, Tina hopped onto the elevator behind him and stood next to him.

"Good morning," he said to her.

Tina pretended not to hear him. Instead, she looked at him with distaste.

"Where've you been? Have you been sick?"

John didn't respond to her question. When the elevator stopped on Tina's floor, she turned to face him and said, "Guess I'll see you later."

"Yeah, uh, Tina, we need to talk."

The doors of the elevator closed, terminating their unrelenting glares. John entered the lobby of his floor, and his staff rushed out to greet him. Gloria followed him into his office and closed the door. She gave him all his missed messages. Before she left out of his office, she informed him about Tina going around questioning everyone about his absence. She had started an office rumor insinuating that she and John were a couple. He called downstairs and asked Ruthie to tell Tina he needed to see her.

Tina didn't hesitate to sashay directly into John's office. He stood up and pointed to the chair for her to take a seat. She sat in the chair in front of his desk.

"What's this all about, John?"

"Tina, we need to talk, but I don't want it to be here. However, I do need to know why you were inquiring about my absence."

"The last time I saw you, you seemed angry with me. I thought I did something to upset you."

"Nevertheless, we need to talk away from this office. Can we meet to discuss the situation? Just to reiterate what I already told you: I'm in a happy relationship. I hope the man you are looking for will find you—"

"Really, John? You don't mean that." Tina crossed her legs.

"Tina, I do."

She stood and stared at him as he eased from his seat.

"Nope. You don't mean that because you *are* the man I was looking for, and I am happy to have found you."

John's lips parted a few times, but he couldn't seem to let any words escape. Tina noticed.

"Close your mouth, baby. Are you available Saturday?"

"No, I have an engagement Saturday. Just set another time and let me know ASAP."

Tina stared at John for a minute and then walked out of the office. She went straight back to her floor. She didn't say anything to anyone in the outer office area as she passed them, went into the conference room, and slammed the door. She walked around the table and laughed uncontrollably.

"*He must be out of his mind,*" she said aloud. "*He had sex with me. Does he think I give a damn about his lady?*"

Tina kicked and overturned chairs, and flung folders all over the floor. She couldn't control herself. Her knees weakened, and she needed to sit down. She slowly walked over to the nearest chair and took a seat.

He's my man and the sooner he realizes it, the better things will be.

When John remembered Tina hadn't set up a day and time for their meeting, he became anxious. He wanted to get this issue with her over— something that shouldn't have happened anyway. John planned to take Sasha out for dinner and propose to her. But he needed his mind clear of Tina.

John reached for the phone to call Tina, but it rang before he could dial her number.

"Hello," he answered.

"John, it's me," Tina said. "Are you still not free to meet with me Saturday? I was thinking we could meet at Don Pepe in Newark around seven P.M.

"I had plans, but if Saturday is the only time you can meet, I'll postpone what I have to do. Sitting down with you is urgent. She will understand."

"Really, John, your invisible woman?" Tina shook her head and hung up on him before he had a chance to say anything.

John stared at the receiver before he set it down. Only minutes later, L.C. strolled into his office, closed the door, and sat in the chair facing John. All John could do was smile. He had an idea what L.C. wanted.

"Man, what's going on between you and Tina?"

John shook his head and stared at his desk. "Nothing."

"Nothing?" L.C. sat straight up in the chair. "She destroyed our conference room, calling you all kinds of MF's and SOB's."

"What? That chick is coocoo."

"Last week she questioned everybody in the office about you not being at work. J., you fooling around with a member of my staff poses a problem for me, given my policy concerning personal and domestic relationships."

L.C. was like a second father to John, so John told him about the situation that happened between him and Tina. He really needed to get his thoughts together to speak with his second dad concerning the issue.

"Man, you had to lay a hard limb on that chick. She's obsessed with you. My wife noticed that shit the night we were at David and Buster's."

"I didn't initiate sex with her. I was asleep, and the next thing I knew, she rode me like she was a rodeo queen."

"Okay, so tell me this: And please don't mistake this as me excusing you, man, but did you enjoy the ride?" L.C. burst out in loud laughter.

"Hell no. We are meeting Saturday to end this mess once and for all."

"J., you are one of the best attorneys in New York City, so I expect you to clean up this shit before Tina is the downfall of your personal and professional life."

"I know. I appreciate you listening. You know I wholeheartedly respect your opinion."

"You are like a son to me. I wish this hadn't gone down between the two of you, but I'm going to be honest with you. You should have taken advantage of the rodeo queen and let her ride that bull all night. Things wouldn't be any worse." L.C. left John's office, laughing.

John didn't think the situation was funny, but he was sure that by Saturday, it would be resolved. He worked late and was tired when he walked onto the elevator. The elevator stopped on the second floor, and Tina stepped on.

Although John was the only person on the elevator, she stood next to him. Tina waited for John to step out of the elevator and followed close behind. As he got closer to his car, he recognized Tina's car parked next to his. He hesitated, and then looked back at Tina and shook his head.

After getting into his car, he put the gear into reverse and looked back in time to see Tina standing behind his car, waving. He stomped on his brake, rolled the window down, and asked Tina what was she doing behind his car. Tina simply waved and shouted.

"Can't a lady say goodnight to her Boo?"

John rocked his head back and forth in disbelief. He wondered what the sources of Tina's erratic behavior were. She was so damn devious and cunning.

John shook his head and then drove off in the other direction, leaving Tina there. He couldn't believe what he witnessed. John was in disbelief about how and why a woman as intelligent as Tina exhibited such extreme, obsessive behavior.

Michael

9

Though terribly angry with Sasha, Michael couldn't stop thinking of her. Sasha was more beautiful now than when she was younger. In replaying the events of Saturday night in his head, he was optimistic about the possibility of him and Sasha getting back together. He wanted to invite her over for dinner, so they could talk about what happened at Don Pepe's but looked around his apartment and said aloud, "Not in this mess!" He needed a housekeeper as soon as possible.

Michael poured himself a drink of Grey Goose and cranberry juice, sat in his recliner, and turned-on Teddy Pendergrass, "Turn Off the Lights." He fell asleep and began dreaming about the date with Sasha. Suddenly, his dream became a nightmare because there was Tina and another guy in an intense argument.

His pager buzzed, stirring him out of his sleep. Michael had an emergency at the hospital. He rushed to shower and get dressed, and then drove to the hospital. On the ride, Michael realized that he hadn't been dreaming. Those events actually happened.

"Damn! Am I really being used?" he questioned himself.

Michael remembered his conversation with Sasha as he drove her home that night. He was livid with Sasha because he felt exploited. He raised his voice at her.

"Damn right, Sasha, you know for yourself that Tina is a drama queen, especially when it comes to a man. You have witnessed her behavior with guys since she started dating in her teens."

"I know, Michael, but she is trying to get herself together."

"How? Trying to introduce a man to you who stated in a restaurant filled with customers that he was *not* her man—oh, and after he had previously made that clear to her."

"I don't know what to believe." Sasha was torn.

"I know this: she needs help. She is a beautiful, intelligent, young woman who is needy for the attention of men. She has some serious insecurity issues, and you are the one who can convince her to seek some counseling."

"What am I supposed to do?"

As Michael came to a stop outside Sasha's place, she opened the car door, but Michael remained inside.

"Michael, I can't tell her she needs help. She will never talk to me again." Sasha got out of the car.

"She's not the only one," he snapped as Sasha stood outside.

She gasped. "Michael!"

"I'll watch you get inside your house."

Sasha slammed his car door and stood staring at him through the windshield in disbelief. He rolled down the window and shouted to her.

"Sasha, go inside before I leave you standing here in this damn parking lot."

With that said, Sasha continued to stand flabbergasted, and Michael made good on his word and drove off.

That was a memory Michael wished he could take back. Michael pulled into his parking space at the hospital and shook his head trying to clear his mind. He wasn't sure what the emergency was about, but he needed his mind clear of the bullshit and drama. He worked twenty-eight hours straight before he was able to go home. He was exhausted and dragged himself into his bedroom. He fell across his bed and slept off and on for the next three days. He got up only to eat and relieve himself in the bathroom.

The ringing of his phone woke him up, it was the chief of staff from the Cardiologist Dept. at L.A. hospital. He asked Michael if he could come as a consultant for a high-risk case for a couple of days. Michael agreed to go, but he needed two days to take care of some business. He sat up on the side of the bed, checking his phone. There were several missed messages and calls from Sasha.

He began dialing Sasha's number but stopped himself and ended the call before he pressed the last number. Michael walked into the bathroom and looked at himself in the mirror. He didn't like the man he saw. He felt silly, running after Sasha whenever she needed him. He was no longer that teenager who worshipped the ground she walked on. He called his barber instead and made an appointment for later that evening.

He showered, dressed, and went to IHOP for some pancakes. While there he called a cleaning service and set up an appointment for someone to clean his apartment. The guys in the barbershop talked about relationships and Michael listened. On his drive home, he thought about his feelings for Sasha. He decided to take advantage of his time away and try to do some soul-searching.

Michael looked at himself in the rearview mirror and said, "I'm not a bad-looking man. I take my health seriously, workout, and work hard. I can't turn back time, but I can let go of the past and look towards the future." He smiled, headed home, packed his bag for L.A., and made himself a drink—this time with Grey Goose and apple juice. He settled down and watched TV.

The doorbell rang. It surprised Michael as he had fallen asleep. He walked to answer the door and found the cleanup crew. It took them two hours to make his apartment sparkle and smell like Ocean Wave by Carol's Daughter. Michael walked from room to room. He could hardly believe his eyes. His first thought was to call Sasha and invite her over.

He shook his head and yelled out loud, "What the hell is wrong with me?" He picked up his bag, walked out of the house, and threw his bag in the trunk of his car. He decided to take a drive to Ruth's Chris Steakhouse in Secaucus, NJ. It was quiet with a romantic atmosphere. Michael's waitress was beautiful with a pretty smile, and she flirted with him. She slipped her name and number on the back of his receipt.

Michael enjoyed his dinner and gave her a big tip. He noticed the writing on the bill and smiled when he saw it was her personal information. He thought, *Damn, man, you should've asked for her number first. Your ass has been out of the dating game so long, you have no swag.*

Michael drove to JFK Airport and went inside the lounge to wait for his flight to be called.

The server came over, told him her name, and asked if she could help him.

"Sure. I'll take a granny green martini with grey goose, please."

She smiled. "My kind of man—like it smooth and cold with a lot of heat."

Michael was flattered. "Sho' you right."

Michael enjoyed flirting with the young woman. He stayed so long, he had to run to catch his plane as it was being boarded. He told the young lady he would be back to see her in a few days.

As Michael sat on the plane, he smiled from ear to ear. He couldn't believe he flirted with two beautiful women who weren't Sasha, and it felt good. A burst of laughter came quickly from his lips. He shook his head as to clear away old cob-webs. He thought, *Damn, I had a cleaning service to clean my apartment of clutter, and now, it seems I'm at the beginning of decluttering my entire life. I thank You, Jesus.* Michael began to hum "One Day At A Time Sweet Jesus." Michael believed better times were ahead for him.

John

10

John arrived home. He went inside his town-house, walked into the living room, and plopped down on the sofa. He rolled his head back and forth in disbelief as Tina crept into his mind. John bounced from the sofa, headed into the bathroom, and took a shower. He made himself a sandwich and poured a shot of cognac. He felt better and decided to turn in for the night.

The next morning, John left for work early. He was in a great mood, so he stopped to buy breakfast at IHOP for everyone. It took three servers to help take the food to his car. He arrived at the office earlier than he normally did.

It was seven A.M. when he arrived at the office and the hallway was empty. John called the security guard to help take the food up to the third floor. He had several bags. When they entered the elevator, they had to set a couple of bags on the floor. John pressed the button for the third floor. Before the doors of the elevator closed, a hand stopped the doors. John's eyes widened and his mouth flew open when Tina stepped inside the elevator.

He wondered what she was doing there so early. He wondered how she knew he would be there. He leaned his back against the elevator and closed his eyes, feeling as if Tina had placed a tracking device on his car. He was beginning to think she was capable of anything. Tina rode to the third floor with John and the security guard. When the guard returned to get the last bag from the elevator floor, he noticed Tina had it in her hand.

She offered him a polite smile and said, "Thank you. I got this. You can leave now."

John overheard her talking to the guard. "Thank you, man," he turned and told him. "Come back later to get breakfast."

The guard nodded and left. John went into his office, leaving Tina behind. She rushed in after him and was about to fuss, but Gloria walked in.

"Good morning, Gloria," John said. "Please set up the food in the conference room and let everyone on both floors know to come for breakfast."

John asked Tina and Gloria to give him a moment, and he closed the door behind them. He walked around the office shaking his head. John felt Tina was smothering him. He needed to get his car checked for tracking devices and to calm his nerves.

John left after the morning conference with a client. He took his Mercedes to the service department and called his father for a ride. Two hours later, the service department called for him to pick up his car. When his father drove to the shop, Dave, the serviceman, stood outside next to John's car.

Dave met John and his dad with something in his hand the size of a quarter.

"Man, you were right. There was a tracking device near the front tire on the driver's side of the car. It was recently installed. It was good you discovered it early."

John Henry rubbed John's back and encouraged him to calm down. John shook Dave's hand and thanked him. He hugged his dad and thanked him also before leaving. John realized he had time to go back to his office to get some more work done. He walked into the building and remembered it was lunch hour.

Tina was waiting for the elevator, so he tried to make a beeline for the stairs. But he was too late. She spied him and held the door open. Although it was full, he squeezed in and took the elevator to his floor. John walked into his office with Tina on his heels.

"Does your invisible woman know about our affair?"

"You're delusional. Get the fuck out of my office and stay out. We're going to settle this madness on Saturday."

John called L.C. and asked that he give Tina the next four days off with pay.

The days were long, it seemed that Friday wouldn't come fast enough. John took Sasha to a movie, and after the movie, they went back to her condo. She asked if he would be available to go to dinner with her the following night to meet her best friend's boyfriend. He said couldn't make it because he had urgent business to tend to.

John wanted to put Tina in her place once and for all. He didn't like the position it put him in with Sasha. He always told her the truth and shared quite a bit with her, but telling her about the drama with Tina might cost him the woman he loved. He promised himself that as soon he settled things with Tina, he would tell Sasha everything.

He tossed and turned all night. Tina couldn't be trusted. John hoped that he could get through to her.

John stayed home all day Saturday, trying to relax his nerves. He was more apprehensive the closer it got to the time. He showered, dressed, and left for the restaurant at seven P.M.. Tina wasn't there when he arrived thirty minutes later, so he sat at the bar and had a shot to release more tension.

John was about to look for her when she walked through the door with a smirk on her face.

"How long have you been waiting?"

"Since seven-thirty. That was the time you gave me in email."

"No, I told you eight o'clock, but that's not important. Let's see if our table is ready." Tina turned to walk away and then turned back. "By the way, I invited my friend and her guest, so I reserved a table for four."

"Tina, why did you do that? I told you that we need to talk. I don't know what you think this is, but I'm not up for meeting your friends. You and I need to have a very serious conversation about what happened."

"And we will once they leave. Now play nice," she said through tight lips then rolled her eyes as she turned to walk away.

Once the hostess escorted them to their table, John asked her to pardon him as he needed to go to the restroom. He needed to gather his composure more so than relieve himself. The nerve of Tina—how dare she invite two more people to dinner with them. All-in-all, he would do what she asked and just play nice because by the end of the night, he would make it abundantly clear to her to stay away from him.

When John came out of the restroom, Tina waved to him. He saw that her friends had arrived, but since their backs were to him, he needed to take his seat to make an introduction. However, no introduction was needed. Tina's friend was none other than Sasha—the love of his life. His stomach did a flip and landed in knots. All hell broke out. Tina was hysterical, and Sasha was in a state of shock. He watched Tina run out after her performance, and another man took his woman home. John was left in the restaurant confused.

He couldn't believe Sasha was Tina's best friend, and that she was there with another man. John finally got himself together and left twenty minutes later. He was still in a daze as he drove home, wondering how in the hell he allowed Tina to destroy his future with Sasha.

Michael

11

When Michael moved back to the New Jersey/ New York area, he was excited about his move. However, his excitement was mostly about the idea of possibly reuniting with Sasha. Over time, he realized the mistake he made when he left her years before. He wasn't sure if she was still single or married with a family of her own. He wanted another chance, but if Sasha had moved on, he would have to opt for her friendship.

He logged on to the Internet to search Sash Accounting Agency, hoping to at least find her office number, but was surprised to see she also had the same cell number. He picked up the phone to call Sasha, but decided to wait. An hour later, his hand shook as he waited for Sasha to answer the phone. He swallowed hard when he heard her soft voice.

"Hello, baby. How are you?"

There was a brief pause as Sasha was stunned to hear Michael's voice. She nearly dropped the phone.

"I'm fine, but I'm in the shower. Can I call you back?"

"Please do."

Sasha didn't say anything after that. She just hung up.

When Michael didn't hear from Sasha, he was disappointed. He looked her up online and found an address. He figured he'd just have to pay her a visit. The next morning was Sunday, so he fully anticipated she'd be home. As he stood in front of her door, his phone rang.

"Good morning, sleepyhead, are you still in bed?" Sasha asked.

"Actually, I'm not." He couldn't help the huge smile plastered on his face.

"What are you doing?"

"Thinking about taking you to brunch. Would you go?"

"Oh, Michael not today. I'm too tired. I'll take a raincheck though."

"Wow. You don't want to see me?"

"It's not like that, Michael. I'm just really tired."

Before Michael could say anything else, Sasha's door pulled open and there she stood, dressed with hair and make-up fully done. She paused with her mouth opened. They were both so in shock that they stood, staring with their cell phones up to their ears. Michael was the first to speak.

"Tired, huh?" He still hadn't lowered his phone and neither did she.

"Um, sort of."

Michael hung up his phone and placed it in his pocket. "Good to see you, Sasha. I guess I'll be going now."

He turned to leave, but she called out to him.

"Michael, wait," she said. He turned to look at her. "I'm actually really hungry. I was going out for a bite to eat."

"So, is it okay if I join you?"

"Of course."

"I mean, I wouldn't want to interrupt any-thing—"

Sasha locked her door then turned back to him. "Let's go."

Sasha hopped in the car with Michael, and they went to an all-you-can-eat brunch spot then ate any and everything in sight. On the way back to Sasha's place they were too full to chat. Once they arrived, Michael invited himself inside Sasha's home, but she did not mind the company.

He sat on the sofa and asked if they could talk for a bit. She sat next to him and nodded, giving him the lead.

"Sasha, our relationship did not end up the way it should have, and yes, I know it's my fault, but I've changed. I'm a few years older, and now, I know what I want out of life and who I want to spend my life with. I've missed you, Sasha, and I'm asking for a chance to prove it to you."

"We can't go backward, Michael."

"No, I'm not asking that we do that. I'm asking if we can start over?"

"Life doesn't work that way. You can't just break up with me, move away without a formal goodbye, and then show back up years later asking for another chance."

"I understand. So, may I ask to start off as friends? You know that was something we should have done from the beginning."

"I wouldn't mind it if we just remained friends."

"Are you seeing someone?"

"Why? Can't you accept that I am just saying no because that's what's good for me, and not because of another man?"

Michael stood in front of Sasha, took her hands and pulled her off the sofa. He lifted her chin, so that they were looking into each other's eyes.

"You're a good woman, Sasha, and I knew I fucked up the moment I got on that plane. You didn't deserve how I ended things, and I can't really blame you if you never take me back."

Sasha's eyes welled, but she refused to let a tear drop. He kissed her lightly on her lips, and then turned and walked to the front door. Sasha slowly trailed him.

He opened the door and then stopped. He looked back at Sasha.

"If your friendship is all I can have, then I'll take that, and I will cherish it."

Sasha lifted her hand and waved a subtle goodbye as he backed out of the door. She closed the door, walked over to the window, and watched as Michael got in his car and drove away.

On the way home, all Michael could think of was his time with Sasha. She was still the life of the party with her silly jokes. He picked the phone up several times to call her, but didn't want her to think he was pressuring her. He took a hot shower instead, settled back in his recliner with a Granny green apple martini, and watched some TV.

An hour later Sasha called Michael. He looked at the caller ID, and he answered the phone on the first ring. He was thrilled that Sasha called. They talked for hours, discussing their past, present, and a few their plans for the future. They also laughed at silly things they did together, and it felt good. Michael told Sasha he was going to Washington on business. He was hoping she would agree to go out with him once he returned home. Little did he know that Sasha would be the first to make the call for dinner plans.

Michael didn't like the fact that Sasha insisted they were just two friends going out for dinner and for him not to get any ideas. The part she didn't tell Michael was that she had a man who was more than a friend. In fact, she was madly in love with him, and that man was Glenn.

Sasha

12

More than a week passed since Sasha experienced the life-changing fiasco at Don Pepe's. She wasn't sleeping very well. Her mind constantly raced with thoughts that broke her heart over and over. It seemed everyone and everything around her was falling apart. She knew Michael was upset with her. He didn't answer his phone when she tried calling him after he dropped her at home. She finally gave up after calling one last time during the middle of the week. She also tried calling Tina that Sunday morning, to no avail. Tina still hadn't reached out to her either.

Sasha realized for the first time in a long while that she was alone. There was no one to call. She kept herself busy the following weekend by cleaning her shoes and clothes closets. She rearranged the kitchen cabinets, vacuumed the carpets, and mopped the kitchen floor. She was so tired that she took a shower and got in bed at eight-thirty. Sasha tossed and turned most of the night and on through Sunday. She gave up on sleep at four o'clock Monday morning. She got out of bed to prepare for work.

She went into the kitchen and made herself a hefty breakfast with coffee. Sasha couldn't eat, so she had two cups of coffee and listened to Glenn's messages. Her heart ached even more. She hadn't realized so many tears flooded her face. She had to redo her makeup before she could walk out her door. She shuffled to her car.

There were hardly any cars on Route 80 East. This was an unfamiliar scene to her, given she was used to driving in bumper-to-bumper traffic. She made it to work half an hour early, and then sat in her car and turned the radio up loud enough to drown out the thoughts parading in her head. Sasha asked herself what had she done, and whether she would be able to correct her mistakes. She was so absorbed in her thoughts that she didn't hear Betty knocking on the window.

"Ms. Sasha, are you okay?"

Sasha shook her trance and turned to Betty. She rolled down her window. "Yes, Betty, I'm okay."

"Can I get you something?"

"No, Betty, go on inside. I'll come in soon."

Sasha sat in the car and tears continued to roll down her cheeks. She felt lonely. She wished she could do something that would take away her pain. She slumped over and wept. Betty came back outside to check on Sasha and found her slumped over her steering wheel. She was scared and ran back inside Sasha's office. She searched the desk drawer for the extra set of keys to Sasha's car and condo.

Betty picked up the desk phone and called another co-worker to let her know not to come in. She also asked her to let everyone know to take the day off. She locked the office and rushed back to Sasha.

Betty helped Sasha to the passenger side of the car. She got in on the driver's side and drove away. Sasha looked over at Betty and said, "Thank you."

"Shush, baby girl. We will talk later."

Betty began to sing "Amazing Grace." Sasha looked at her and smiled. She remembered as a little girl her mother sang that song to her and Kellie. She drifted off to sleep.

Betty woke Sasha up and helped her inside her bedroom. Sasha sat on the bed. Betty then went into the kitchen placed the kettle on the stove to heat water for tea and went back into the master bathroom.

Betty ran a bubble bath for Sasha and then lit the candles next to the tub. She called for Sasha to get in the tub. As she waited for Sasha, she noticed the CD player nearby and thought, *hadn't seen one of these in a while*. Betty leaned over and then pressed play. Najee's "Butterfly Girl" began to play.

Sasha stepped into the bathroom and began to undress as Betty closed the door behind her. She went into the kitchen and prepared a light snack for them to eat.

Betty placed the food and drinks on a tray and took them back into the bedroom. Once Sasha got out of the tub, she stepped into a pair of pajamas Betty left in the bathroom with her. Betty placed the tray on the bedside table and pulled a chair close to the table. Sasha stepped out, refreshed, and calmed.

"Sasha, it is time we talk. I am concerned about you."

Sasha plopped on the side of the bed. "Betty, I feel so alone. Thank you for your support."

"But why and how? Two weeks ago, you were all smiles and happy when you came into the office. You were so giddy. We were all thinking that you were pregnant."

Sasha giggled because she recalled that was the weekend she had spent with Glenn at his home.

"Betty, I had the most exciting weekend with Glenn. It was the first time he made love to me. He was romantic: brought me flowers, and took me to a jazz concert, and dinner. Then, he took me back to his home. It was like a picture in Southern Living Magazine—just beautiful.

"He led me into his bedroom, the covers were thrown back, the bed was covered with red roses, and a bottle of champagne was set up near the bed. We undressed each other, and oh what a night."

"Girl, you have me in a sweat over here. So, baby, why are you in this state of depression?"

"It was all good until I hurt my friends and caused them pain and mistrust. My best friend thinks that I am sleeping with her man and my ex-boyfriend is angry because he thinks I used him."

Sasha didn't feel like she could rehash the events. She felt like a fool and more tears flowed down her face. Betty walked over and cradled Sasha in her arms.

"Baby, it will help to talk about it and get it out."

"My best friend wanted me to meet her new man and invited me to dinner. I asked my ex, Michael, to be my escort, but I didn't tell him I had a man or that he couldn't make it. Michael thinks my best friend, Tina, has some serious character flaws. The dinner ended up in disaster. When Tina's man came from the men's room and sat down, it was my Glenn and her John."

Betty couldn't hide her surprised reaction. She cupped her mouth with her hands.

"Oh, no, Sasha."

"Yes. He denied they were a couple, and she ran out of the restaurant. My ex grabbed me, and we left Glenn sitting there."

"Sugar, how did you feel when Glenn said they weren't a couple? Had he ever lied to you before?"

"No! We spend a lot of time together. I never thought of him as a cheater."

"Are you still in love with Glenn?"

"Yes, I am."

"Do you want to mend your relationships with your best friend and your ex?"

"Yes, Betty! Tina has been my ride-or-die friend since elementary school, and I still believe Michael and I can be good friends. At least, that's what I would like."

"Baby, how are you going to mend your broken heart?"

"I haven't thought much about myself."

"What do you think you need to do?"

"I'm not sure, but I'm sure you will tell me."

"You are going to pull yourself together, pray about it and follow your heart. You have to fix yourself first, Sasha, before you can fix the issues you have with others."

"Now let's eat."

They ate and laughed at things that happened at the office over the past years. After cleaning up everything, Betty called her husband to pick her up on his way from work. Sasha was feeling better. She hugged and kissed Betty as she left.

"Thank you. See you tomorrow," Sasha told her.

"No, I will see you on Wednesday. You need to rest and call me if you need me," replied Betty.

Sasha

13

S asha did exactly what Betty suggested. In fact, she took the rest of the week off work. She prayed and fasted for the next four days. Sasha prayed for forgiveness for the hurt and pain she had caused to others and herself. She asked for clarity, strength, directions, and for God to order her words and steps.

She woke up early Saturday morning and on her way into the bathroom she noticed the date on the calendar. She couldn't believe how much time had gone by since the incident in the restaurant, and Sasha thought it was time for her to call Tina. They had been friends since third grade, and no way she was going to let a man destroy that.

She picked up her phone and dialed Tina's number, but the phone kept ringing. She was about to put the phone on the kitchen counter when there was a knock on her door.

Sasha yelled, "Hold up."

When she opened the door, there stood Tina. They looked at each other for a couple of seconds.

"Come in, Tina. We have to talk about what happened."

They went into the living room and sat across from each other. Sasha started the conversation.

"Glenn and I started dating almost seven months ago. At first, I thought he was gay because he never made a move on me."

"Oh, hell, stop right there," Tina demanded. "John never used his suave moves to get you in bed?"

"No," Sasha said. "We didn't get intimate for six months."

That tidbit of news put a little smirk on Tina's face. She thought about the night she took him home and waited for him to fall asleep. Then, she took the initiative to go into his bed and get busy with him. She couldn't understand why he waited so long to be intimate with Sasha. She wondered if his wait was about how much he really cared for Sasha. Tina was upset, but she knew that Sasha was truly a loving person, and it would be hard not to care for her.

Sasha just wanted to clear the air and be over this confusion.

MATTIE WARD

"Tina, what's done is done. I don't want to lose your friendship because of Glenn, so I gave him back the ring."

"He gave you a ring?" Tina was crushed.

"Yes." Sasha stared intently at her friend.

Glenn proposed to Sasha only days before the big fallout, and she accepted. She had planned to tell Tina, but once they discovered they loved the same man, Sasha's news was placed on hold. Tina had more questions.

"So, you've seen John since that night at the restaurant?"

"No. Well, not exactly." Sasha shook her head. "I still can't believe your John was my Glenn." She sighed.

Tina was anxious for more answers. "I know, right? So, how did you give him back the ring?"

"I waited one morning inside the building across the street until I saw Glenn pull into the parking garage. I waited about fifteen minutes before crossing the street. As I approached the building, I saw him through the window. His back was to me as he entered the elevator."

Tina's heart sank. She wondered if Sasha saw her hopping on the elevator with him to flirt. Tina hadn't missed many opportunities to be on the elevator at the same time as John.

"Was he alone?" Tina asked.

85

"No, there were people getting on the elevator at the same time, which helped him not to see me as he turned around. I had on a pair of sweats, a hoodie, and sunglasses. I slowed my pace and didn't enter the building until I saw the elevator doors close."

"Oh, that was smart. So, how did you give him the ring?"

"I placed it in a wrapper and then put that in a large manila envelope before I left home. I asked the first-floor receptionist to call him down for a package. I waited until she hung up and said he was on his way, and then I watched as the elevator numbers descended to the second floor before darting out. I ran back to my car in the garage around the corner without looking back."

"Wow, Sasha. That's deep. I can only imagine how you must've felt after that." Tina paused then took a deep breath. She had another pressing question on her mind. "Have you ever been to his apartment?" she blurted.

"Um, yes, I have. He took me to his house, too."

"Oh? I never went to his house, but I heard it was the bomb. So, how was the sex?" Tina knew it was a bit much to ask, but she couldn't help herself.

"Just as you had experienced: it was the royal fuck of my life."

There was a brief silence, but then the two friends began to laugh so hard that they started crying. They embraced and wept on each other's shoulders. Before the night ended, they vowed to tell each other the name of any man they dated from then on. They realized their friendship was stronger than any man in the world. Tina left just before dark.

That night, Sasha praised God for things going so well between her and Tina. She genuinely loved her friend and couldn't imagine losing her. She asked God for the same results with Michael once they talked.

Glenn left Sasha messages daily. She was confident that whenever she decided to answer him, he would still be willing to talk to her. But this wasn't the time. Sasha thought of Glenn and how much she couldn't shake her feelings for him.

She watched TV in the living room for a bit and then decided it was time for bed. She stood to go into the bedroom, but suddenly, she fell back in her chair and begin to cry. She missed Glenn terribly. She wished she could at least speak to her sister Kellie. Kellie would know how to comfort her. This was the first time she said a silent prayer for her sister in years.

Lord, please forgive me for the terrible things my sister overheard me say about her. It has been six years since I last saw or heard from her. I need her sisterly bond, and I realize now how much I want her to be a part of my life. Please let her forgive me. Amen!

Michael

14

Michael was extremely busy since the last time he saw Sasha. He was angrier with himself than with her. So, he threw himself into his work. He had been in L.A. for two weeks, assisting in a hospital. While there, he met with his friend, Edward, who is a psychiatrist.

"Hello, Michael, it has been a long time since I saw you. So, what brings you here today? Is it professional or personal business?"

"Man, this shit is personal. A few weeks ago, Sasha, my ex, invited me to accompany her on a dinner date with her friend. I happily accepted the invitation even though I never really liked this friend. When we arrived at the restaurant, everything went downhill from there."

Michael continued to share the details of the night at Don Pepe's with Edward listening intently. Michael didn't realize how much he really needed to get off his chest. After about ten minutes of straight talk, Michael finally took a breath so Edward could interject.

"Well, Mike, that's quite a story. I heard you had moved back to the East Coast, but I didn't know you and Sasha were dating again."

"Man, we are not a couple. I wanted us to rekindle our friendship and see where it could go from there. But damn there's no chance of that unless she breaks up with Glenn or John, or whatever his name is. Sasha was going to meet Tina's new man John, but he was Glenn—the guy Sasha was dating at the same time. All of that drama was so embarrassing, and I'm angry as hell with Sasha for using me as an ornament. I thought I didn't mind being her date that night, but after finding out about her man, I feel used."

"Okay, Mike, I'll start with you and your role in the situation."

"Man, what are you talking about? I'm not involved in no damn drama."

"Calm down Mike. Listen and learn."

"You stated that you wanted a friendship with Sasha, but are you dating anyone else?"

"Hell no, man, I'm working long hours at the hospital and traveling back and forth between the East and West Coasts. To be honest, I really don't have time for dating."

"So, Mike, you're telling me that you're too busy to date, but you sent your representative to respond to Sasha when she needed you to fill in as a substitute? Then, 'Mike', 'the man', got upset when the representative's feelings got hurt?"

Michael paused to think. "Man, that shit is deep. Why did I ever come here? I knew you would go hard on me like this."

"Just hear me out. It happens often, especially at the beginning of a relationship. We want the other person to see our representatives, who is a false identity of our real selves. The representative gets tired of role-playing, and when the real person shows up, the relationship is destroyed before it gets started."

"Man, I was so damn mad, I left her pretty ass on the side of the road, and I haven't answered any of her calls."

"Mike, you went to the East Coast and reintroduced your representative, but when things got tough, the real man got in his feelings. You need to call Sasha and apologize for your immature behavior. Didn't you tell her you are a different man now?" Edward struck an emotional chord with Michael. Michael dropped his head as Edward continued. "Talk to her and be honest about how she made you feel that night. Then, shake off the dust, and find yourself a nice lady to date."

"Damn, man. I knew I needed to talk to you today."

Michael did a brief shimmy and then brushed the tops of his shoulders. He and Edward laughed at his gestures.

"Don't laugh, Ed. I'm starting right now— shaking this shit off. I hurt her when I broke up with her, so I guess I just have to eat this one. She got me back."

"I don't think she was trying to get you back, man."

"Yeah, I know."

"So, where is Sasha's family?"

"Her mother and father are deceased. Sasha was angry with Kellie, her sister, and said some nasty things Kellie overheard. Kellie walked away, and I don't think Sasha has seen or spoken to her since."

"Aahh, so this could be why Sasha refuses to say anything to Tina about her behavior. She's afraid Tina might leave her. I'm willing to bet Sasha needs counseling. She might be suffering from Separation Anxiety. After all, her parents left—albeit not of their own accord, her sister left, and you admit that you left her before, too."

"Wow!" Michael brushed his hand across his head. "Bro', I get it. Damn, I didn't mean to be a part of the problem. I fully regret leaving her like that."

"Listen, let me give you some cards of a friend, who is an LPC in the city. He can help both Sasha and Tina."

Michael reached for the cards. "Thanks, man."

"Mike, you have some work to do. Help these women to heal their broken hearts. It might be tough, but you can try to be the glue that those ladies need to rebuild their relationship. You might benefit from talking to my friend, too."

"I hear ya. I'm going to do my best."

On the drive to the airport, Michael was in a stupor over everything Ed helped him realize. He speed-dialed Sasha. He tapped the steering wheel waiting for her to answer.

"Hello, Sasha we need to talk."

"Michael, I'm so glad to hear your voice. You haven't returned any of my calls or messages."

"I've been in Los Angeles for two weeks, and I just wasn't ready. I'm on my way back. I'm heading to the airport. I do want to talk to you."

"Yes, please. I want to clear the air, Michael. What time will you get in?"

"My flight will land late, and I have the early shift at the hospital in the morning. How is Tuesday evening work for you?"

"Let's meet at Applebee's around five-thirty. Is that good for you?"

"Sure, I'll see you Tuesday."

"Good night, Michael. Have a safe flight."
"Good night, Sasha, and thank you."

Sasha

15

M ichael and Sasha both had a long Monday and were glad that they chose Tuesday to meet. Sasha was early and was seated in a booth in the back of the restaurant. When she saw Michael, she stood and waved him over. His first reaction was to lean over and kiss her, but he stopped himself. Edward's comments were in Michael's head, so he opted not to kiss her and took a seat instead.

"Should we order first?" asked Sasha.

They ordered food and while they waited, Sasha started the conversation.

"Michael, I'm so sorry about getting you involved in the mess at Don Pepe's. I had no idea myself. I'm still trying to figure things out."

"Sasha, I met with Ed while I was in L.A. I was so damn angry with you, and I needed to understand my anger."

"You had every right to be angry, Michael."

"That's what I thought, too." He laughed. "Ed made me see that I shouldn't have been there in the first place. I returned to the East Coast not only for my new position at the hospital but to win back your heart."

"Michael, I didn't know."

"Yeah, I know. See, when you suggested we remain friends, I told you that would be fine, but I was truly hoping you would see the change in me soon, and give me another chance. I was trying too hard and let my guard down. I couldn't question you about the night we were blindsided. In fact, all of us were shocked at the outcome of the evening."

"Ain't that the truth."

"Still, I can see your heart belongs to dude, and I want to find someone to love me as much as love him. I will always be your friend, Sasha, but I need to venture back into the dating game."

"I understand, Michael. But are you saying we can't be friends?"

"Don't worry. If you need me, I'm available. I will be here. Now let's talk about Tina. She has always shown obsessive behavior with guys, and you made up excuses or turned your head to keep from acknowledging it. She needs you to help her, and I'm willing to help, too."

Michael reached into his pocket and pulled out the cards that Ed gave him.

"Ed gave me this card to give to Tina. It's the business card for a counselor in the area. Ed thinks it would be helpful for Tina to have some type of therapy to get to the root of her problems."

Sasha had a lump in her throat. She had many things running through her mind, but she hardly knew how to respond. She sipped her glass of water before saying anything.

"I know Tina has issues, but I'm worried that she will be mad at me if I suggested counseling."

Michael shrugged and patted Sasha's hand. "Do with that what you will. Now as for you, lovely lady, have you been in contact with Kellie?"

Sasha almost spit her food on Michael. She didn't say anything, but Michael could see her eyes watering.

"It's time that you reach out to her. You need her, Sasha. She's your sister, not Tina."

"Why do you say that? Tina is just as much my sister as Kellie."

"I know that you and Tina are close, but your blood is Kellie. How would your parents feel, if they were here and knew you and Kellie have no bond?"

"They'd be hurt, I'm sure."

"Exactly. I just know that if Kellie was here now, she would be the one comforting you and letting you know everything will be okay. Tina, on the other hand, has been following you for years. She wants *your* life, but her issues keep her from obtaining the life she deserves."

Michael reached into his pocket, pulled out the same card, and gave it to Sasha.

"Who is this card for?" she asked.

"You, Sasha. It's for you."

"Ed gave me three cards. He said our problems needed to be fixed. We are all grieving from something, and we need help. I'm ready to let go of my grief. Are you, Sasha? You can call and meet with Tina. If you need my help, call me."

"I lost my appetite. Let's get some take-out trays, and I don't want to hear any more of your nonsense, Michael."

"Sasha, give up the act. Call the counselor and try to find your blood sister."

Michael sat like a solid statue as Sasha leaped from the table and ran out of the restaurant.

John

16

A couple of weeks passed since John had seen or talked with Sasha. He called her number at least a few times a day, but like all of his previous calls, he got her voicemail. This day was just like the others. He called and left her another message, stating he missed her and would love it if she'd call him when she got a chance.

After work, he sat in his dark living room, listening to the Temptations, "Ain't Too Proud to Beg," with a bottle of cognac, a glass, and lemons. He took a sip from his glass, closed his eyes, and relaxed in the recliner. His thoughts went back to the time he surprised Sasha with her favorite food.

What is Sasha doing, he thought. *And who was that guy with her at the restaurant? Surely, no one she is dating.* John knew he messed up by not sharing the drama, Tina, an office worker, caused him from the beginning. He figured it was something he could handle on his own without involving Sasha. He hoped Sasha could forgive him and give him a second chance.

John just wanted a chance to explain the situation to Sasha. He never lied to her. He never said anything about Tina because it wasn't anything to tell. Sasha was the one he wanted in his life. After all, he was honest with Sasha in the beginning when he said he was searching for his wife.

John sprung up in his chair, reached for the cognac, poured himself another drink, and gulped it down. He stood and walked around the room, thinking how happy Sasha was when he proposed to her. John plopped back down into his chair, head in his hands, and then he remembered his conversation with his dad.

"Son, do you love Sasha with all your heart and soul?"

"Yes, Dad. I love her and want to marry her."

"Then, my son, you fight to get her back."

John hopped from his chair and looked at his watch. It was seven-thirty P.M.. He grabbed his jacket and keys, rushed to the back door, and then into his garage. He was on his way to see Sasha. He pressed the button to lift the garage door and was startled when he saw Tina standing there.

"What are you doing here, and how did you get into the gate?" he fussed.

Tina struggled to stand straight as she was a bit tipsy. "I knew you would be lonely, so I came to see you. You gave me the code when I drove you home, remember?"

"Tina, I need you to leave here now. I'm on my way out."

"Oh, are you going to see your ex? Sasha? Did you know she's dating Michael?"

The remark about Sasha dating someone else hurt John to the core. He leaned against the inside of the door to steady himself. His knees felt as if they were about to collapse. Tina could see from his reaction she had hit the bull's eye with this tidbit of news. She raised her right hand, exposing a bottle of cognac in it.

"I brought this bottle, so we could drink while we discuss your dilemma, or should I say *our* dilemma?"

"It's time for you to go, Tina. We have nothing to talk about."

"Oh, you not only have something to discuss with me, but you also have something to *do* with me!"

John asked Tina to leave again, and when she refused to go, he turned around to go inside his condo. By now, she had blown his high. As he was about to enter the apartment, Tina began to yell.

"Help! Someone, please help me!"

John ran and grabbed her arm. He yanked her into the apartment and slammed the door behind them. He was furious with her. Tina could see it in his eyes, but she had a smirk on her face.

"What is wrong with you making a scene at my place? What the hell is your problem?"

"You are my damn problem."

"What?"

"I rode your ass like a cowboy does a bull, and what you do? You stopped talking to me. But you took Sasha to your house, and you fucked her all night, and that's what I want, John. As your woman, I should be the one you treat like that."

John had no words. He stared at Tina as she plopped down at his table and took a swig out of her bottle. He looked at her with empathy. Though he had never made a pass at her, the pain of losing someone you care about he understood very well. The night Tina was talking about, he was intoxicated and did not reciprocate their tryst intentionally.

He went into the living and poured himself another drink. He didn't trust Tina or whatever she had in that open bottle. He sat down and sulked for an hour before he realized Tina was dead silent. He went back into the kitchen and found her fast asleep at his table. He took the bottle of cognac out of her hand, and held it up to the light. He saw white particles attached to the bottom. He had no idea what it could be.

He was angry, but he needed to get her out of his apartment. He checked his watch, and it was ten P.M. It was late, and he needed help. The only person he knew to help him was his dad. So, he called him.

"Dad, I have an emergency, and I need you. I'm in New York."

"Give me thirty minutes, Son," his dad replied without further questions.

John Henry arrived at the condo in exactly thirty minutes. He knocked on the door and John opened it for him. This was the time for his dad to ask questions, but John shook his head to stop John Henry. All he wanted to do was get Tina home.

John searched her purse, found her car keys, and walked until he found her car a block from his condo. He pulled her car next to his car, and John Henry helped put Tina on the passenger side of her car. John Henry got into his car and followed his son to New Jersey to Tina's parents' house.

John used Tina's phone to call her sister and explained the situation. She met them outside and helped get Tina into the house. John and his dad rode in silence until they were back at the condo.

"Son, who was that, and what happened?"

"That was Tina, Dad. She came here with a story about Sasha, and she brought a bottle of cognac, laced with a substance. She intended for me to drink it, but she did, and it knocked her out."

"What about Sasha and you, son?"

"I was on my way over to see if I could talk with her when Tina arrived unexpectedly at my door. She made a scene, and I allowed her to come into the condo." He looked at his dad and said, "I love Sasha, and I will get her back."

They were tired and went inside the condo. John gave his bed to his dad, and he took the sofa. They would finish their conversation over breakfast.

John had been ecstatic with the direction of his life before the fiasco with Tina. After the breakup with his ex-girlfriend three years before, whose insecurities were the cause of their breakup, he prayed God would help him find his virtuous woman. He knew Sasha was the one God had destined to be in his life. John was content in his soul, and he was going to do whatever it took to get Sasha back.

Sasha

17

$\mathbf{A}$nother long day came and went with more thoughts of Glenn. As much as Sasha wanted to, she couldn't shake the fact that she still loved him. Sasha picked up her mail from the mail center at her condo and then drove home. When she walked in, she decided she would finally listen to her voicemail. It had been weeks since she even peeked at them. She clicked to listen to the recordings and was informed she had several missed messages. Her heart skipped when she realized most of them were from Glenn.

"Hmm," she said, thinking about the romantic times they had together.

She melted with every word of his messages. He missed her, too. She felt she could at least call him just to see how he was doing.

She picked up the phone and dialed the number, then hung it up, not sure if it was an appropriate time.

"Maybe not now," she said aloud.

Sasha sat on the sofa then looked over the mail she brought in. There was a letter with no return address. She opened it, and to her surprise, it was from Kellie. It had been six years since she and Kellie even spoke. Kellie was the oldest, full of spunk, and outgoing. Kellie disappeared after the harsh words she heard Sasha say at their mother's funeral. No one knew whether she was okay after their mother died.

Sasha read the letter and was pleased to find out Kellie was doing fine. She learned that Kellie was married to a wonderful man named Travis. They were parents to a two-year-old daughter named Kiya. Kellie left a number at the bottom of the page with a plea, stating PLEASE CALL ANYTIME. IT'S BEEN TOO LONG, AND I WOULD LIKE TO TALK WITH YOU. ALWAYS, YOUR SISTER, KELLIE.

Sasha had mixed feelings and didn't know what to think, so she called Glenn—who always reasoned with her when she needed to talk about her sister. He knew about what happened with Kellie from their long talks about family members. He answered on the first ring.

"Sasha, baby, is this really you?" His tone was one of desperation.

"Yes, Glenn. I know I've been avoiding you, but now we need to talk."

"Okay. I'm ready to talk, too, babe."

"Listen. We'll get to everything else, but I just need to talk, and I had no-one else to call. Can you come over please?"

"I'll be there in twenty minutes."

Sasha sat down and waited with tears in her eyes, remembering the fight she and Kellie had before she disappeared. *Will she ever forgive me for all those nasty, things I said?*

Sasha read Kellie's letter over and over, trying to figure out if there was any ounce of forgiveness in it. Before she had time to fully relax, there was a knock on the door. It was Glenn. She went over to let him in.

"What's wrong?" he asked as soon as he stepped foot inside.

"Have a seat, Glenn."

Sasha walked over to the sofa and sat next to him.

"My sister, Kellie," she said then paused. Sasha was full of emotions and could hardly get the words out. Her tears strangled her voice. "She wrote meeeeeeee a lettt . . . ter."

"That's great, Sasha. Is she okay? Do you know where she is?"

"No, the letter didn't have a name or return address on it, but she left her number."

"That's odd."

"Well, she stated in the letter that she hoped by not addressing the envelope, I would open the letter. Should I call her?"

"Sasha, that's your only sister, and from everything you've told me, you really love her."

"But what if she hasn't forgiven me?"

"You can't take back the words that Kellie overheard, but the fact that she reached out to you tells me she might be willing to accept an apology."

Sasha agreed with him, picked up the phone, and stared at the number on the letter. John slid closer to Sasha and rubbed her back as she nervously dialed the number.

"Hello, Kellie," Sasha said.

The lady on the other line stated, "No, this is Rose. I'm the nanny. I have Ms. Montgomery's phone while she is taking a bubble bath. I'll take the phone to her now. May I tell her who is calling?'

Sasha paused and swallowed before stating, "I'm her sister."

The woman asked Sasha to stand by while she and the baby go to the master bath and give Kellie the phone. Kellie's voice was vibrant and loving when she spoke.

"Hello, Sash, how are you doing?"

"I'm fine, Kellie. How're you?"

"Wonderful. I'm so glad you decided to call."

"Me, too, Kellie. It's well-past time we talk."

"I agree. When can we get together and have lunch?"

"I'm ready when you are. Where are you?"

"My family and I live in D.C., but we have an apartment in New York. How about I bring Kiya, so she can meet her aunt? Would that be okay?"

"Yes, that will be fine. I'm looking forward to meeting my niece. I know she's as beautiful as her mom."

"Actually, Sash," Kellie began, using the pet name she used when they were growing up. "Kiya looks just like you."

Sasha was so surprised by Kellie's remark that she was speechless. She couldn't say a word until Kellie called her name.

"Did you hear me, Sash?"

"Yes. I'm stunned. Does she really look like me?"

"Yes. She has your eyes and your gorgeous long, beautiful hair. As she grows, she's more like you than anyone else." They both laughed. "Well, I'll give you a call Friday, Sash, to let you know what time we will be arriving Saturday, okay?"

"All right, Kellie, and thank you so much for reaching out. I'm looking forward to seeing you."

When Sasha got off the phone, she gave John a big hug and thanked him for being there.

He asked if they could talk about what happened between them. Sasha had a look on her face as if she didn't hear him.

"Can we talk please?" he stressed.

Sasha was hesitant for a few minutes and finally said, "Ok. Go ahead. I'll listen."

"Sasha, I never had anything going on with Tina. Our relationship was always professional. I know she says otherwise, but I always made it clear to her that I was not interested and that I had a woman."

"But something just doesn't add up, Glenn. What am I missing here?"

"Nothing, baby. I promise. I told her from the very beginning of her working at our office that I didn't date within the workplace. In fact, that is one of our office rules."

"Why did she think the two of you were a couple?"

"Because she became obsessed with me. The fact that I was in a great relationship didn't faze her. I told her I was profoundly serious about the woman I love."

"And who is this woman, Glenn?"

"Sasha, you can't be serious. You know it's you. I should have told you about Tina the moment I knew she was a problem. Can you forgive me? I love you, Sasha, and I want to spend my life with you and only you."

Glenn took Sasha's hand and kissed it.

"Please tell me you still love me, Sasha."

With tears in her eyes, she softly said, "I never stopped loving you, Glenn."

They embraced each other and held on as if it was for their dear lives. But Sasha realized she still didn't understand something else. She broke their hug and looked at him.

"How and why in the world does Tina call you John?"

"I'm sorry I never explained this to you before, babe. Glenn is my middle name. It is my family's legacy to name the boys John. My great-great grandfather's first name was John, and on his deathbed, he made his wife promise that all males born into this family would have the first name John."

"So why wouldn't you just tell me your name was John?"

"In the office and my professional life, that's who I am, but my parents and friends all began calling me Glenn to distinguish me from my dad and brothers. I planned to be as close to you as possible, so I wanted you to know me as Glenn."

Though Sasha understood his reasoning, it still didn't take away the fact that the name mix-up caused problems. She loved him, and she wanted to believe everything he said, so she told him they could start over.

It was getting late, and they both had work the next day. As they kissed goodnight, they became heated and eventually retired to Sasha's bed for some much-needed and warranted make-up sex. Sasha was glad she called him over. Her man proved he certainly loved her. He made up for all of the lost time.

Sasha

18

Friday night Kellie called to let Sasha know the time she and Kiya would be there. Sasha was excited to see Kellie's number on her cell.

"Hi, Kellie, are you still coming?"

"Yes, we will be there shortly. I will give you a call when we get settled in the apartment. Talk to you soon." Kellie seemed excited as well.

Ten A.M. came and went, so Sasha was worried. *Why hasn't Kellie called yet?* She hoped their flight wasn't delayed. While Sasha's mind wandered, the phone rang. She saw that it was Kellie, so she hurried to answer.

"I was starting to worry," Sasha said without saying hello.

"Why?" Kellie responded. "I told you once we settled in, I would call. What time do you want to meet and where?"

Sasha was relieved to hear Kellie and Kiya were okay. "Are you guys hungry?"

"Yes, a matter of fact, we are. What do you suggest?"

"How about some Chinese food?"

"That sounds great."

"Okay. We can meet at Red Dragon Restaurant at two o'clock," Sasha decided.

Sasha arrived at the restaurant fifteen minutes early. She wanted to get a good table facing the entrance of the door. She was excited to see her niece for the first time and her sister after several years. Six years was a long time, and she hoped Kellie hadn't changed too much.

Sasha saw Kellie and her beautiful niece as they entered the restaurant. She stood to get their attention. They walked over to the table. Kellie gave Sasha a big hug and introduced her to Kiya. She picked her up and gave her a big squeeze as if she didn't want to let her go. Sasha bought Kiya a little porcelain doll.

They had lunch, talked about the past, forgave each other, and realized what was done, was done. After lunch, they went back to Sasha's place.

"Sash, I'm really glad to be here with you. I missed you all these years, and we need to get together more often."

"Indeed," Sasha agreed. "We certainly should."

Sasha and Kellie were ecstatic over their reunion. Acting like two little kids, laughing, talking over each other, and telling jokes. Both discussed how the six years of separation had affected their lives. Sasha and Kellie listened to each other speak from their hearts without resentment.

For the first time, Sasha could hear and understand the hurt she caused her sister. She had been selfish all the years she never tried to reach out or locate Kellie. Sasha was grateful that Kellie forgave her and wanted to make up for the lost time. The two sisters shared stories of the events in their lives over the missed years. Sasha looked over at Kiya as she played with her new doll. She told Kellie that Kiya was a wonderful child. She even wondered if Kiya would be open to staying over with her sometimes.

"When can Kiya spend the night with me?" Sasha asked.

"First, let her get to know you, and then we will take it from there."

The sisters reminisced about their childhood, and Sasha shared with Kellie that she was in a loving relationship with someone. Then, Sasha invited Kellie to have dinner with her and Glenn later. Kellie accepted. Sasha also wanted to hear about how Kellie met Travis.

"Sash, after I graduated from college, I moved to D.C. and was hired at Walter Reed Hospital as an emergency room nurse. I was so lost. I spent most of my time working, trying to forget the harsh words I overheard you say to Tina. Six months later, Travis, a Staff Sergeant in the Marines ended up in the E.R. after being in a car accident. He was admitted and became my patient. Two months later, we started dating, and the rest is history."

They both giggled. There was a knock on the door. It was Glenn. Sasha was surprised to see him because he knew she was spending time with Kellie and Kiya. She invited him to come in and introduce him.

Glenn smiled and said, "It's a pleasure to meet you."

Kiya ran up to Glenn and hugged him as if she knew him.

Kellie looked from Glenn to Sasha and asked if she could speak with her for a moment. As soon as they went into Sasha's bedroom and closed the door, Kellie questioned her about her beau.

"Gurl, that man is fine as hell. Is this the gentleman you mentioned earlier?" Kelli asked.

"Yes, and what I didn't tell you is that our story is a long one." Sasha dropped her head and smiled.

"Believe me: I have all the time in the world. So, get to talking." Kellie sat on the bed and crossed her legs.

"Well, it's like this: I love him, and I know he loves me, too. He asked to marry me, and he gave me a beautiful diamond ring."

Kellie gasped and then swung her eyes to her sister's ring finger. "When's the wedding?"

"I gave him back the ring because there were some issues that needed to be resolved. But we are back together. That's why I want you and Travis to have dinner with us tonight. I want you to get to know him."

Kellie stood to hug her sister. "Well, hopefully, there will be another engagement sooner rather than later. He seems like a keeper."

Sasha was proud to have Kellie's approval. They hugged then headed back into the living room. Kellie decided it was time to leave Sasha with her man for now. She would see them later on for dinner. Kellie gathered their things and called Kiya over to leave.

Kellie and Kiya were leaving when Kiya said, "I'll be back, Uncle Glenn."

Sasha and Kellie looked at each other in amazement. When her sister and niece left, Sasha couldn't wait to question Glenn about Kiya's response.

"Where did Kiya get that?" Sasha folded her arms across her chest.

Glenn smiled then went over to have a seat on the sofa. "Well, I have a way with kids. Kiya and I bonded while you and Kellie were in the other room. I told her she could call me Uncle because I'll be her Uncle Glenn soon."

"Oh, is that right? Someday soon, huh!" Sasha sat next to him.

"Of course. No doubt in my mind. How was your day with Kellie and Kiya? Are you relieved to reconnect after years of waiting?"

"Yes, I'm relieved. Kellie forgave me for being an asshole."

Glenn and Sasha sat, talking for hours, and before long, it was time to get dressed for dinner.

When Sasha and Glenn arrived at the restaurant, Kellie, Travis, Glenn's parents, and brothers were all seated waiting for them. Sasha was surprised to see everyone. She turned to Glenn, looking for an explanation.

Glenn pulled out Sasha's chair. "Oh, I forgot to mention that since we would be bonding with your sister and her husband, I figured it would be a wonderful time to introduce my family to everyone."

"Oh, Glenn, how nice of you." She took her seat.

Dinner was going to be a perfect night for Sasha. Before dessert Glenn stood to address everyone.

"I have something to say."

He looked at Sasha and got down on his knee. Kellie gasped and covered her mouth. Tears formed in her eyes. Glenn's parents and brothers were equally pleased to witness the moment.

Glenn pulled out the two-carat, oval-cut diamond ring he originally proposed to Sasha with and asked her to marry him. Sasha was overjoyed.

All she could say was, "Yes . . . Yes! I will marry you, Glenn."

Sasha had a flood of tears rolling down her face. She looked over at Kellie. Kellie cried, too. She was so happy to be a part of this day. Sasha continued crying as she spoke through tears.

"God sent him to me," she told Kellie.

"I know, Sash. When is the wedding day?"

"February fourteenth—Valentine's Day," Glenn replied before Sasha could say anything.

"It will be cold then," Sasha stated. "But I guess that doesn't matter as long as we are warm in heart." Sasha started crying again. "Valentine's Day—what a perfect day to get married."

It was late October, which allowed her a few months to plan and prepare for her big day. She wanted to call Tina, and she let it be known.

"Oh, where's my phone. I need to call Tina to let her know I'm engaged again."

Everyone looked shocked once those words came out of her mouth. Kellie was the first to speak up.

"Why do you want to call her right now? Sash, this isn't the time. You know your friend can be full of drama. Just continue enjoying this moment with your husband-to-be and new family."

Glenn agreed. He touched Sasha's arm softly and said, "Boo, can this wait until later?"

All the while, Sasha had dialed Tina's number, and the line was ringing. Sasha paused just as Tina answered, wondering if she had done the right thing.

"Hello," Tina said for the third time.

Glenn and Kellie just stared at Sasha as she eventually began to speak to Tina.

"Hello, girlfriend," Sasha said, hesitantly. "It's been a minute with no hear from you, so I wanted to give you a shout."

"What's up, Sasha. How are you?" Tina was a bit confused about the noise in Sasha's background.

"Fine, and you?"

"Living well. I'll be moving into my new house two months from today."

"That's wonderful." Sasha cleared her throat before saying, "I have some good news myself. Glenn asked to marry me again, and I said yes." There was an awkward silence between them for a moment. Sasha continued. "I'm calling because I want you to be my maid of honor. Oh, and more good news! Kellie is here!"

Tina was stunned. She didn't know Glenn and Sasha were dating again and simply couldn't believe her ears. She composed herself long enough to pretend she was excited for Sasha.

"So, he's the one, huh?"

"Yes, Tina, he's the one."

"Do you trust him?"

"Tina, what are you getting at? Glenn and I have hashed things out, and what we discussed is none of your business. You're still my best friend, and I just want to know if you will be a part of my wedding?"

Tina was surprised at Sasha's firmness. Sasha never spoke to her in a harsh tone. Tina swallowed her pride and responded kindly.

"Gurl, you know I wouldn't miss being in your wedding for anything."

Sasha was upset with Tina for asking questions about her relationship with Glenn. She was determined not to let Tina or anyone else ruin her relationship with him. Sasha told Tina the wedding would be on Valentine's Day, and that Kellie would be her matron of honor and her niece the flower girl. All of this was shocking news to Tina.

"Seems as though you got it together," Tina said.

"Not quite, but I will. Let me get back to everyone. I just had to let you know the good news. Talk to you later. Bye, Tina."

Sasha hung up before Tina could say anything else. She still wasn't happy that Tina questioned whether she and Glenn should get married. When Sasha looked up, all eyes were on her. She glanced around the room and wondered why everyone stared.

"What's up?" Sasha questioned.

Kellie had never heard Sasha defend herself with Tina. She was proud and amused that Sasha stood up for herself. Rather than answer Sasha, everyone carried on as if nothing happened.

Tina

19

T ina was furious. She slammed her phone down on her bed. *What the hell is going on with Sasha. Has she lost her damn mind? She took my man. Now her sister reappeared after years of missing in action. They're all at dinner, witnessing John propose to Sasha for a second time, but I wasn't even invited.*

Tina shook her head and sweated profusely as she plopped on her bed. She couldn't believe this bullshit. John was *her* man, and if he was going to marry anyone, it would be her. Sasha, her ride-or-die, had the audacity to be all happy and called to asked her to be the maid of honor in her fucking wedding. Then, the bitch got irritated when she questioned her about the groom and wedding.

Tina hopped off the bed then went into the kitchen to pour herself a stiff drink. She had to devise a plan to put a stop to this wedding, but she also wanted to play it cool. She still needed Sasha and Kellie to help her move to her new place. But someone would pay for her agony.

Tina made herself another drink, took a seat on the sofa, closed her eyes, and began to scheme. She decided to call Sasha. The phone rang four times before Sasha answered.

"Hey, gurl," Tina sang in Sasha's ear. "I hope I'm not calling too late."

"Oh, no girl, I just hung up with Glenn. I'm too excited to think about sleep now."

"Sasha, I'm so happy for you. When can I see that gorgeous ring?"

"I'll send you a picture of the ring now. It's beautiful, Tina. I feel so lucky to have Glenn back in my life and to marry him."

"I feel you, girl. I feel the same way. Oh, wait, the picture of the ring just came through." Tina paused to open her text. She gasped. "It's beautiful, Sasha. Hey, can we talk later?"

They were both silent for a moment. Sasha was taken aback. Tina had called her, but now she was ending their conversation abruptly. Tina had to end their conversation before Sasha could hear her cry. Tina was distraught over the engagement, and now this damn picture of the ring sent her into more emotions. She had to face the reality that her man and Sasha were really going to get married. Tina realized her relationship with Sasha was at risk, but she loved John, and she would do anything to have him to herself.

If Tina got John to make love to her again, they both would lose Sasha. But, if she allowed him to marry Sasha, she would lose Sasha to him. Tina leaped out of her chair. She was numb as she saw her lifelong friendship with Sasha crumble before her eyes. For the first time during their friendship, Tina had to admit to herself that she was jealous of Sasha.

She felt Sasha was ahead of her in every phase of their life. Sasha always had the good guys. She owned a business, bought a condo, and she could afford all the luxuries in life she wanted. Tina felt she always had to play catch up to Sasha. Now Sasha was going to marry the man she wanted. It was John's fault Tina threw herself on him. He shouldn't have ignored her advances in the first place. But John wanted Sasha, and he gave her everything. Even though Sasha ditched him without a second thought, the renewal of their engagement proved he was still waiting for her.

Tina wanted to make him pay. She fell asleep in a drunken stupor. When she woke up, she got dressed and went to Walmart that night. Tina went straight to the jewelry counter and found a ring similar to the one in the picture Sasha sent her. She placed the ring on her left ring finger and walked out of Walmart with a smile on her face.

This was the first step in her plan. Tina had to wait. She needed Sasha and Kellie's help to move. Then, she would put part two of her plan into action. She got into her car to head home when her phone buzzed. It was a message from her realtor who left her some good news.

Tina peeped at the message and saw she needed to call her realtor to set up a time for a final walk-thru of the house and sign the contract. She could be in her new home by the first week of the next month. Tina pulled to the side of the highway. Tears ran down her face, but she smiled and clapped at the same time.

She felt the move was a blessing and a new beginning. If she could have John share this new beginning, her life would be complete. She composed herself and then drove home. Once inside her apartment, Tina picked up her phone to share her good news with Sasha but ended the call after glancing at the time.

The wall clock displayed it was midnight. Tina decided it was too late and that she would call Sasha the next morning. She prepared for bed. She closed her eyes and dreamed about marrying John. She even envisioned their families coming together at the new house on Thanksgiving Day.

Tina

20

T ina was up early for work. She took her time to make sure her makeup was perfect, and her clothes accentuated her shapely petite body. Once she arrived in the parking lot, she glanced down at her left finger and smiled. She got out of the car and sauntered into the building. The elevator was closing, but someone held it open for her. She slid back into her usual spot—next to John, of course. She bid him good morning.

"Good morning, John." She winked at him.

He was shocked that Tina wasn't smothering him as she normally did. In fact, she gave him plenty of space. He nodded and just watched as she got off on her floor without looking back. When she entered the office, there was chatter going around about John's engagement. Tina wanted to gag, but Ruthie came running up to her.

"Hey, Tina, did you know John got engaged?"

"Ruthie, of course, I know." Tina flashed her left hand.

"O-M-G, girl, you are lucky. Why didn't you tell me? Tell me more!"

"Girl, you know it's against company policies, so it's a secret for now."

L.C. noticed Ruthie holding Tina's left hand, so he walked over to see what was going on.

"Ladies, what's going on over here? Is this a private party?" He looked back and forth between the ladies.

Tina spoke up. "Nothing really. Ruthie was just admiring my new nail polish."

Ruthie walked away, leaving Tina to deal with that situation. L.C. noticed how Tina fidgeted.

"Tina, are you okay?"

"I'm fine, L.C. I couldn't be better." She smiled then started around him. "Excuse me. I'm on my way to congratulate John on his engagement."

"Okay. I'll let you go."

Just as Tina waved goodbye to him, L.C. saw the ring on her left hand. He hurriedly went into his office and picked up the phone.

Tina went straight to the third floor and stopped by Gloria's desk. She wasn't much in the mood for small talk, but she stopped anyway once she spotted John on the phone. After several minutes, she couldn't take anymore.

"I'm sorry, Gloria, but I really need to touch base with John, so I can get back to the second floor."

"Okay. Talk to you later."

As Tina walked up to John's office, his eyes were on his computer as he spoke on the phone. She stood off to the side and listened.

"What do you mean she has an engagement ring on?" John said into the receiver. He paused to listen. "Hell no! I'm not aware of her getting engaged, and if she is, she's not engaged to me."

Tina peeped around into John's office and noticed him totally engrossed in the conversation on the phone. She pulled back just before he looked up. He had no idea Tina was just outside the door listening.

"Yeah. I saw her in the lobby talking to Gloria. She was probably showing her that fake-ass engagement ring." John had to laugh himself. "Listen. I have lots to catch up on. I'll talk with you later, man."

Just after John hung up the phone, Tina, rounded the corner and knocked on the door. John was surprised, but not really. He beckoned her in and motioned for her to have a seat. He remained behind his desk.

"Why are you here, Tina?"

"I'm here to congratulate you and ask if I can take you out to celebrate."

"After all, we are engaged. I mean, we both are engaged."

"What do you mean, 'we'? Who are you engaged to, Tina?"

"Oh, you wouldn't know if I told you. Anyway, how about lunch?"

John knew Tina must've been up to no good, but for entertainment purposes, he accepted her invitation. He had every intention to let Sasha know about it though.

"Where would you like to go?"

"We can go down to Applebee's." Tina stood and then stepped around the desk in front of him. "By the way, I would like a celebratory hug?"

Before John could reject her, Tina placed her arms around his neck, making sure the onlookers saw their embrace. He jumped out of his chair and pushed her away.

"Look, Tina. I know I said yes to lunch, but it really depends on my schedule."

Tina sashayed toward the door and then paused. "Twelve o'clock—Applebee's," she said sternly.

Tina returned to her office and called Sasha to invite her to lunch. Her scheme was working just as she'd planned. She made Sasha feel as though lunch was all about celebrating her engagement to John. Sasha agreed to meet her at twelve-thirty at Applebee's.

Tina sat back in her chair and bellowed at the thought of what was to come. At 11:45, she called John's office and made him aware that she would meet him at the restaurant. She left early to stop by the florist. Tina purchased a beautiful bouquet of red roses with a balloon that stated, I LOVE YOU. She arrived at the restaurant only ten minutes before L.C. walked in. When she noticed him heading toward her, her mouth dropped open. It took a minute or two before she could say anything. L.C. was amused by her reaction. He silently chuckled as he took a seat. She finally questioned him.

"Where's John?"

"Oh, he's coming. He had to park his car."

"Okay. I didn't know you were coming, too."

Just then John wandered to the table. "L.C., move over, man. I'll sit next to you."

Tina was furious. The server came over with the menus and asked for their drink orders. Once the drinks were ordered, Tina excused herself to the ladies' room. She pounded her fist against the wall, cussing and wailing as she pranced around in a circle. She composed herself and then headed back toward the table. She rounded the corner where her table was but stopped when she noticed Sasha had arrived.

Tina noticed the surprised look on the men's faces as Sasha stood in front of them. John stood to greet his bride-to-be.

Sasha leaned in and gave him a kiss. "Baby, what are you doing here?"

"I was gonna ask you the same thing. Tina invited me to lunch to celebrate our engagements. Apparently, she's engaged, too."

Sasha took note of the roses and balloons at the corner of the table. "What?" She shook her head. "Tina invited me to lunch to celebrate *my* engagement. She never once said she was engaged. Where is she?"

"In the ladies' room." John nodded toward the restroom area.

Sasha turned and saw Tina. Tina immediately started towards them. L.C. got up and gave Sasha his seat then whispered in John's ear, "Man, you're fucked."

Tina sat down, and L.C. sat beside her. The server returned with their drinks and asked Sasha if she wanted to order a drink. She refused, but L.C. downed his in one gulp and then asked the server to bring another round for the three of them. Sasha just wanted to get to the bottom of what was going on.

"Tina, what is this all about? You're engaged? Who's the lucky man? And why didn't you tell me that you invited Glenn here."

Tina felt interrogated. She took a deep breath. "I don't have to tell you everything that is happening in my life. I simply invited John to celebrate with me."

"You and Glenn celebrating your engagement?" Sasha couldn't believe her ears. "Listen, Tina, we are not playing this game again. Glenn proposed to me—*not* you."

John was just as baffled as Sasha. "Tina, what games are you playing?" He released a deep grunt. "You lied and tricked me to come here. What happened to your man—the one who brought you the roses?"

The server handed L.C. his drink and sat the others on the table. This gave Tina time to think. She was caught in a web, but she came out fighting.

"John, you brought the roses and balloons for me."

L.C. spit his drink all over his clothes. He couldn't believe Tina lied with a straight face. She held her left hand up for Sasha to see. Sasha had a knot in her stomach. She couldn't believe it. She glanced back and forth from Tina's ring to hers and noticed how similar they were.

Sasha turned to her man. "Did you propose to her?"

"He couldn't have," L.C. said, coming to his friend's defense.

Sasha acknowledged L.C. for the first time. "Who are you? What do you know about this mess?"

"I know J. loves you, and he proposed to *you*. What I have heard here from Tina is disappointing. I'm quite disgusted she would hurt you with these lies and wreck her friendship."

Sasha felt rage like never before. "My best friend wouldn't do this to me! I don't know this person standing here." She eyed Tina and then looked at Glenn. "Enjoy your celebration."

Sasha walked out of the restaurant. Glenn slid from his seat to go after her."

"J, let me have your keys, man."

John hurriedly tossed the keys to L.C. and then sprinted from the area.

"Go after your future," L.C. yelled behind him.

He turned his attention to Tina and shook his head. Her attention didn't part from John as he ran out the door. L.C. took another gulp of his drink and then set the glass on the table hard.

"Tina, you are suspended—indefinitely. I will be in touch as to whether you can return to the office."

Tina could have blown smoke from her head. L.C. stood and grabbed the keys. He walked out, leaving Tina sitting there.

Sasha

21

Sasha slumped over the steering wheel of the car to sob. She hadn't noticed Glenn when he walked up. His heart went out to her as she cried uncontrollably. He tapped on her window. She jumped up in her seat a little as he startled her.

Sasha sat up and dried her eyes, and then lowered the window. "Go away, Glenn."

He tugged on her door, hoping it would open. "Sasha please open the door. We need to talk."

"I don't want to talk. Just go away."

"Baby, I'm not leaving here until we talk. I'll create a scene in this parking lot if I have to."

Sasha looked around and saw that people stared in their direction. She unlocked the door on the passenger side.

"Get in," she said reluctantly.

Glenn got into the car and turned to face her.

"I know Tina is your best friend, Sasha, but she has a severe problem. I don't know why you can't see that she can't be trusted."

"I'm starting to see that now, but how did you ended up on a lunch date with her?"

"I didn't want to have lunch with her, but I decided maybe I should see what she was up to. I asked L.C. to come along as my go-between to help keep her in check. Listen, babe. I'm not sure if Tina is aware of her problem, or if you have observed her behavior lately, but something has to be done."

"What do you mean? She's my best friend. I just think she got caught up with you, and frankly, I'm finding it hard to believe that there wasn't more to the relationship you had with her."

Glenn looked at Sasha. He wanted to reassure her there was nothing going on between him and Tina. He took her in his arms and held her tight. He decided this was the time to reveal some vindictive things Tina had done to hurt his reputation. He told her everything. She couldn't believe her ears.

"Glenn, I never would have expected any of this from Tina."

"Sasha, Tina exhibits obsessive behavior. She really needs to seek some type of counseling."

"Wow. You're not the first person who told me that."

"Really? Was it another one of her victims?" he halfheartedly joked.

That was a good question, but Sasha couldn't answer it because Michael was the one who had the same comment about Tina. He never said whether Tina pursued him. She sucked in a deep breath and then turned to Glenn.

"So, what do you want me to do about Tina? I don't want to lose my friend."

Glenn wished there was an easier way to deal with the conflict. He shook his head and tried to put his feelings into words that wouldn't hurt Sasha. He took her hands.

"Babe, I'm not and will never be comfortable around Tina. You see what she just pulled in there," he said, pointing at the restaurant. "Who buys a fake ring, balloons, and roses, then pretends that her best friend's fiancé is hers? She is dangerous, and I will never trust her. I don't even want to be in the same room with Tina."

Sasha had once thought of Tina as a ride-or-die friend. But Tina didn't seem to think of Sasha that way. Tina was jealous of Sasha and her happiness. Sasha was starting to see this. She knew her decision of what to do with her friendship with Tina would determine the fate of her future with Glenn.

"What are you trying to say, Glenn?"

"I love you, Sasha and want to have a life with you, but only if it's Tina-free. She will never let us be happy."

He leaned over and kissed Sasha softly on the cheek. When he pulled back, Sasha released a few tears as she spoke.

"I've been friends with her since third grade! I asked her to be my maid of honor. What do I do with that?"

Glenn dropped his head and stared into his lap. "Babe, please just take me back to work."

Sasha was appalled. She cranked the car and then drove off. Glenn got out of the car before she came to a complete stop in front of the office. He got out without saying goodbye. She pulled off. The more she thought about the conversation with Glenn, the angrier she became. She grabbed her phone from the seat and dialed Kellie's number.

"Hello, Sash, what's going on? Are you okay?"

"I'm okay." She paused and then decided to tell the truth. "Actually, no!

I'm mad as hell with Glenn."

"Slow down, Sash, what are you talking about?"

Kellie could hear that Sasha was agitated and wanted to know what was wrong and where she was. There was something serious happening, and she wanted to be there to help her sister. Sasha felt better knowing Kellie was willing to share her problems. They agreed to meet at Sasha's apartment.

Twenty minutes later, Kellie arrived at Sasha's place and rushed inside. She found Sasha brewing some tea. They sat behind the island to talk.

"I really don't know where to start, Kellie. But I received a call from Tina inviting me to lunch to celebrate my engagement, or so I thought."

"What do you mean?"

"Tina set me and Glenn up. She didn't tell either one of us about the other being invited. And to make things worse, Tina sported an engagement ring identical to mine."

Kellie almost spit out her tea. "Say what? You want to run that by me again?"

"You heard me. Tina had balloons, and roses, and wore an engagement ring that looked just like mine. She stated Glenn purchased all of those things."

Kellie's mouth fell open. She didn't know what to say, so she covered her mouth with her hand.

"I knew Tina had the potential to be dirty, but what the hell? What did Glenn say?"

"He denied everything. I didn't know what to believe, so I walked out of the restaurant."

"Come on, Sash, how could Tina know what your ring looked like?"

"She asked me to text her a picture the last time we spoke."

Sasha continued to share her thoughts on the day's event, but she left out the part about L.C. and what he thought of Tina's shenanigans. In spite of what L.C. said, Sasha was still torn over whether Glenn had done something to lead Tina on and kept her conflicted. Kellie sat there shaking her head, trying to understand her sister's thought process.

"When you walked out, Sash, what did Glenn do?"

"He came after me, and we talked. He told me that we will never be happily married if Tina is in our lives. He doesn't want a relationship with her. He simply refuses."

"I can't say that I blame the man. But, anyway, what are you going to do, Sash?"

"Tina is my best friend, and we've been kickin' it since we were eight years old. You don't just throw away friends like that. I asked her to be in my wedding. There has to be more to her behavior than what it seems."

"Like what, Sash?"

"I don't know. Maybe she still thinks Glenn is leading her on. I'll have to have a talk with her."

"So, you choose to trust Tina over your man?"

"I don't know what to believe, Kellie."

"So, is there going to be a wedding, Sash?"

Sasha's phone rang before she had a chance to answer Kellie's question. She intentionally avoided responding and answered the phone instead.

"Hello, Sasha," the voice on the other line said. "Gurl, you left out so quick I didn't have a chance to give you more good news."

Sasha was dry. "What good news, Tina?"

Kellie moved closer to Sasha when she heard Tina's name. She thought this girl must be on some drugs or that she was plain evil. What news did she have to tell her sister now? Tina was on the phone, acting as if the scene in the restaurant never happened.

"I'm moving into my house in two weeks– on the fifth to be exact, and I'm still gonna need everyone's help. Find some strong men to help with the heavy furniture."

"What?"

"I gotta go, girl. I'll see you then. "Bring John and Kellie's husband, too. Bye."

Tina hung up before Sasha could protest. Kellie looked at Sasha, shook her head, and plopped on the sofa. She couldn't understand her sister's attachment to Tina.

"Sash, you didn't answer my question before the phone rang. Is there going to be a wedding?"

Sasha's eyes went blank just before she fell onto the chair with tears rolling down her cheeks.

She couldn't answer Kellie's question because she didn't have one. She wanted both Tina and Glenn in her life and wasn't prepared to make a choice. Sasha couldn't look at her sister.

Kellie got up, went to kneel in front of Sasha, and took her hand. "Sash, Tina needs help, and it's the kind you can't give her by ignoring all the signs."

"What signs, Kellie?"

"Sash, you said earlier she did some inappropriate things, accusing Glenn of buying her flowers and the same engagement ring that you have. Now she's calling you as if nothing happened. That isn't normal behavior."

"Kellie, she really does have some issues. I can see that now, but I just don't think she is doing anything intentionally to hurt me. She's always had my back."

"Please don't use that lame excuse to let Tina get away with her behavior. She wants your man, and she's using you to get to him."

"What should I do?" A flood of tears fell from Sasha's eyes. "This shit hurts, but I want to be there for her, and see her get the help she needs. Plus, I promised I would help her move."

Sasha listened as her sister gave her an honest perspective. Sasha was clear on Tina and her antics, but she wanted to avoid an altercation. She wasn't ready to acknowledge that her best friend had turned some of her unusual behavior issues toward her. She witnessed Tina display some unpleasant pranks on guys who broke up with her or with some of their new girlfriends.

Now, Sasha had become the one Tina was playing cruel pranks on. Sasha knew she needed a plan to take control of her own life if she didn't want to lose Glenn. She stood and picked up her phone to dial Tina's number. Tina answered on the third ring.

"Hello, Tina."

"What's up?"

"You stated that you need us to help you move in two weeks. I have another appointment on the fifth, but this is what I'm going to do as a housewarming gift to you. Find a moving company to move your things and all expenses are on me. Try Two Men and A Truck. If you need an extra man to help you, get your father to assist you. Kellie and I will come for a couple of hours to help set things up."

"Sasha, what do you mean? I told you to bring John and Kellie can bring her husband."

"No, Tina. Glenn nor Travis will be coming with us. So, take it or leave it. Call me when you're ready to pay the deposit. Also, Kellie and I will come over once your furniture arrives at the new house. Just text me the address.

Sasha hung up without a formal goodbye.

Kellie ran over and hugged her sister. "I'm proud of you. But understand this is only the beginning of your battle with Tina. So, stay strong, sis."

"Oh well. I'm not going down without a fight for my future with Glenn. Tina has always said in other instances, 'may the best woman win,' and in this instance, I *am* the best woman, and I *will* win."

"Let's go to your favorite place to celebrate Sash. I'm starving."

"Red China here we come!"

Kellie was so proud of Sasha, but she was also concerned about her. She knew Tina was vindictive. Kellie hoped Sasha's response to Tina's request would help resolve the issues Tina had with Glenn. Hopefully, Sasha would be able to salvage her wedding plans and Tina would get some help for herself.

Tina

22

T ina was home and mad as hell. She wondered how she could make Kellie disappear again. Sasha seemed to have grown some balls since her sister came back into the picture. She got up, poured herself a drink, and said, "May the best woman win."

Tina couldn't believe Sasha hung up on her. She got up, went into the kitchen, and pulled out a bottle of Johnnie Walker Blue from the cabinet. She grabbed a can of Coke from the fridge then poured herself a drink and said, "I *am* going to be Mrs. John Saunders." The night was young, and she didn't have to return to work for an undetermined amount of time. So, drinking and thinking became her pleasure.

Two weeks later, Tina called Sasha. It was her moving day, and she was beyond tired of Sasha's silent treatment. Tina heard the moving van outside. She walked over to the window and saw Sasha and Tina pulling behind the truck.

Tina pretended to be happy to see Kellie. She swung the door open and stepped out on the porch with her arms wide, ready to give the sisters a big hug. She hugged Sasha first and then reached to embrace Kellie.

"Kellie, it's so good to see you. Where have you been in the last six years? I heard you're married and have a daughter, right? Weren't you the one who said you'd never have children?"

Kellie stared at Tina and played nice for Sasha's sake. She looked at Tina and replied, "Life brings about a change, huh? But we can talk about that later. We're here just to work."

Tina smirked. She knew Kellie had never been fond of her, but Tina didn't care. "Right. Work. So, where are the muscle men?"

"I have no idea where your father is, Tina," Sasha quipped.

Tina's mouth flew open at Sasha's remark. She was at a loss for words, and then she laughed it off. She turned and walked back into the house. This was not the Sasha she knew, and this made Tina angry. As she saw Sasha move about the house, chatting and smiling with Kellie, Tina suddenly felt betrayed.

Kellie and Sasha held hands as they walked through the house. Tina drifted to the window and stared in deep thought for a bit. Then, Sasha and

Kellie spent hours helping Tina unpack and set up. Once they were done, all of the women were tired. Sasha and Kellie stayed for a while to regroup. Tina ordered pizza, and they had some wine.

By that evening, Sasha and Kellie got up to leave. They needed to meet Glenn's mother to look for gowns for the wedding. Tina thanked them for being there for her. She really did appreciate their help.

About an hour later, Tina stood in the window of Valencia's Bridal staring at her best friend and sister along with another woman. Sasha walked about the store pulling out gowns and showing them to the two women. Sasha chose a gown, and then placed one chosen by Kellie on one arm, and another one chosen by the unknown woman across the other arm. Tina decided to go in.

"Kellie, I think I'm really gonna like this one," Sasha said, holding up the gown.

It was white with a V-neck and had lace tulle and beads on the long chapel train. It had three-quarter-length sleeves and an open back with covered buttons at the small of the back.

"It's gorgeous, go and try it on, Sash."

"What do you think, Mrs. Saunders?" Sasha said.

Tina's eyes bucked. *Mrs. Saunders,* she thought. *John's mother is here?*

"Yes, it's beautiful. Go and try it on, Sasha," Mrs. Saunders replied. "I'm sure my son will love it."

The salesperson took the dress from Sasha and took her into a dressing room. The other ladies took a seat to wait for Sasha. As Sasha stepped out of the dressing room, they heard a voice from behind them say, "Sasha, you look beautiful!" It was Tina.

Kellie and Mrs. Saunders looked at each other and then turned their attention back toward Sasha. Kellie was surprised to see Tina there. It hadn't been an hour since she and Sasha left Tina, straightening up her new house.

Everyone, including Tina, were in awe of how beautiful Sasha looked in the gown. It was a perfect fit. Sasha didn't receive a response to their reactions to the gown because as she stared in the mirror, all she could think about is the fact that Tina crashed her fitting. Kellie and Mrs. Saunders ignored Tina and went to look for their pink gowns. Kellie took the liberty to explain to Mrs. Saunders who Tina was. Mrs. Saunders finally could put a face to the infamous Tina.

The women found their pink dresses and returned to the seating area, but Tina came back with a white gown.

"Kellie, do you like my gown?"

Kellie tried to mask her frustration, but it was hard. She pulled Tina aside to talk with her about her gown.

"Tina, why would you choose a white gown, when you know our gowns are to be pink?"

"Kellie, you have been out of the picture for years, so don't you dare question me about anything that I do!"

Sasha came out of the dressing room and asked, "What's going on?"

Kellie and Mrs. Saunders stepped away to look for the flower girl dresses. They walked around the gallery, leaving Sasha and Tina to talk.

"Tina, what are you doing here? How did you know where to find us?"

"I have ways. Why didn't you invite me to join the party?"

"Reservation was made weeks ago. Check your text, Tina. The other ladies received their texts, but your selfish ass ignored yours and decided to move into your new house on the same day. I'm too busy to play games with you, Tina."

"Really, Sasha, or was it that you didn't want me to meet John's mother?"

"Wow! Tina, Glenn never introduced you to his family, and I can't believe you showed me an engagement ring that Glenn never gave you."

Tina didn't get a chance to respond to Sasha's smart remark because Kiya came running up. Travis, Kellie and Mrs. Saunders were close behind her. Travis had just arrived with Kiya for her fitting, and she wanted Auntie Sasha to see the pretty gown she was about to try on. Everyone went over to the dressing area to have a seat. When Kiya stepped out with her dress on, she looked like an angel. She was so excited when everyone clapped and cheered for her.

Mrs. Saunders' and Kellie's dresses were beautiful and fitted them nicely, but needed alterations for the lengths. Tina was the only one who hadn't tried on a dress, so the other ladies left her at the gallery.

Once they were gone, Tina walked over to the counter to chat with the saleswoman.

"Excuse me," Tina said, holding a white dress. "I think I like this one, but is it possible to order it in Pink?"

Tina was determined to have a dress that would outshine Sasha's dress. She really wanted the white dress but felt Kellie would cause a problem for her. The saleswoman checked their system.

"You know what? That might be possible, but I'm not really sure," she said. "I'll have the owner call you with more information."

Tina turned and left the gallery. She had to simmer down, so she drove home in complete quietness. Kellie had angered her with the questions about the dress. She expected Sasha, her running mate, and confidante, to step up for her, but she didn't say anything. Tina didn't like the way things had changed between the two of them. And to top things off, Tina couldn't believe Sasha had walked out of the shop and left her standing there. Tina took deep breaths to calm her nerves. She snickered and yelled, "They will all feel my wrath."

As she pulled into the garage of her new home, her phone rang.

"Hello," she answered.

"Ms. Tina, I am the owner of the bridal Shop. I'm sorry to say we can't find a pink dress similar to the white one."

"Oh, that's fine. I'm the maid of honor, and I spoke with the bride already. She says the white one will do. I'll be there tomorrow to pick it up."

Tina hung up her phone and pressed to lower the garage door. She watched it close and sat in her car, laughing hysterically.

Tina

23

Several months passed, and Sasha and Tina managed to keep their friendship intact. Tina returned to work after the holidays, which turned out to be a sixty-day suspension for her. L.C. was torn on whether to allow her to return, but after another panel interview, it was determined Tina learned her lesson. Though it was hard, she only spoke to John in passing.

February came before Tina knew it. She and Kellie worked together for a month planning the bridal shower for Sasha. They constantly bickered. The things Tina tried to do would sabotage Sasha's shower, and Kellie was determined not to let her ruin it. Kellie didn't trust her and didn't believe she wanted the best for Sasha.

Tina wanted the shower to be at her new house, but Kellie chose a suite at Deedee's Hideaway, a hotel on the Groove in Jersey City. It was convenient for attendees who lived in New York and New Jersey. The suite had five bedrooms and five baths with a huge living room, dining room, and kitchen. The ride to the church would only take thirty minutes.

"Tina, I need you to meet me at the hotel at one o'clock. We need to inspect to make sure everything is okay, and the florist is meeting us there."

"Florist? Why the hell do you need a florist?"

"Why else? For the decorations."

"Decorations? I made some things for the guests and colorful paper flowers.

"Oh, that's fine. We can include your things with the pink and white roses, and balloons."

Tina didn't bother to say goodbye. When she hung up, she broke a sweat as she looked cross-eyed at the phone. She placed the phone on the table and shouted aloud, "What is wrong with this bitch? I'm ready to go Bruce Lee on her boujie ass."

Tina grabbed her things and headed out of the door. She was still smoking mad when she reached the hotel. Kellie waited for her in the lobby. Once inside, Tina was impressed. When she got off the elevator and walked into the suite, she gasped and covered her mouth. It was beautiful. She had little to say to the decorators, but when they finished, she was speechless. She placed her things next to the door, so the guests could take their gifts on the way out.

"What do you think about the place?" Kellie asked.

"Sasha is going to love it."

"Did you bring pajamas with you?"

"No, I have to go by my mom's to get my bag. What about food and drinks?"

"You don't have to worry about anything. We have all the food and drinks needed."

Kellie hired Glenn's sister-in-law to cater the food, two bartenders, and three waitresses, so the food and drinks were covered. Tina took one long look at the room before she walked to the elevator.

Once inside and the door closed, she slid on the floor and the dam inside of her broke. She pulled herself up before the door opened on the main floor and dragged herself to her car. On the way to her parents' house, she became angrier and angrier. This was supposed to be her wedding, not Sasha's.

When she arrived, she went directly to the bar and grabbed a bottle of Johnny Walker Blue, and turned it up. Her mother snatched the bottle from her mouth.

"Tina Miller, what is wrong with you?" her mother yelled.

"I'm celebrating the ruin of my life."

"What are you talking about? Who and what is ruining your life?"

"Sasha! That bitch thinks she's gonna marry John tomorrow. Over my dead body!"

"Watch your mouth, young lady. Have you forgotten who you're talking to? You and Sasha have been friends for years. She would never do anything to hurt you or your friendship. But you're my child, and I know you, so, Tina, what have you done?"

Tina jumped out of the chair. She looked at her mother. "That's right! I'm your daughter, not Sasha."

Tina took the bottle of Scotch with her and went to dress for the bridal shower. When she arrived at the shower the party was live. Everyone was having fun. Some of the women were dancing.

Tina spied Sasha seated in a high-backed chair in the middle of the room, surrounded by other women. She looked as if she was holding court with her servants. Tina held up the bottle of Johnny Walker Blue she'd been drinking from.

"All drinks were on me!"

Everything and everyone seemed to have stopped, except the music. Tina turned and headed to the kitchen. Kellie stepped in front of her and reminded her that bartenders were walking around to take orders.

Before Kellie could say another word, Tina cut her off. "Where's that handsome husband of yours?"

"Where's your man, Tina, or do you have one?"

"He's at his bachelor party." Tina smiled and stared her square in the eyes.

"You're still delusional. You never had a man of your own, have you?"

Tina had raised her hand to slap Kellie when someone came to get them.

"What are you two doing in here?" the woman asked. "The party is revving up now. The stripper is here."

Kellie winked at Tina and walked away, laughing.

The stripper was a hunk and a half. He sat on Sasha's lap and made some moves that made all the women break into sweats—everyone except Tina, that is. She was busy drinking and texting Glenn pictures of the stripper. She also texted him a message.

JOHN IS THIS THE KIND OF WOMAN YOU WANT FOR YOUR WIFE? I'LL NEVER ACT THAT WAY.

John replied back to her, TINA, YOU ARE AN INTELLIGENT, BEAUTIFUL WOMAN. THIS ISN'T THE TIME FOR YOUR B.S. ONE DAY YOUR LUCKY MAN WILL COME ALONG, BUT THAT'S NOT ME. SASHA HAS MY HEART NOW AND FOREVER. PLEASE ENJOY YOURSELF AND LEAVE ME THE HELL ALONE."

Tina walked over to where Sasha was opening her gifts and stood in front of her shaking and crying. Everyone stopped and watched Tina.

Sasha was concerned. "Are you okay?"

"No, I'm not fucking okay. My best friend stole my man, and she's sitting here like she's the queen of the Nile."

"I didn't steal your man, Tina. Why would you say that?"

"I received a texted from John, and he loves me, not you, Sasha."

Kellie had called Glenn and asked him to get there ASAP. There was a knock on the door. Glenn and Travis walked in once Kellie opened the door.

John walked over to Sasha and asked, "Baby, are you okay? What's going on?"

"Did you send Tina a text that you're in love with her?"

"No, I didn't. She sent me messages and this is how I responded to her."

John pulled out his cell phone and showed the messages to Sasha. She saw the pictures and read what Tina texted him. As Sasha skimmed the message, Tina went into a rage. She didn't know what to do. She looked at Sasha with pain etched on her face and a waterfall of tears. Her legs weakened, and she flopped on the floor at Sasha's feet. She looked up and noticed all eyes were on her.

"Sasha, you never had a problem being alone. There always were nice guys in love with you. Everything seems so easy for you. You have it all. When I met John, the amazing man was respectful and so kind to me, and I fell for him.

But he never made a pass at me. When I discovered that you were his woman, I became so jealous of you and afraid that he would come between us. I'm in love with him. I've tried everything to control my feelings, but I can't."

Sasha got up from her chair and slid onto the floor next to Tina. She wrapped her arms around her and rocked her like a mother would rock her hurting child.

"Tina, we have been friends for twenty-plus years. We have shared good and tough times. I love you like a sister, but you have allowed jealousy to place a wedge between us.

I don't want you to drive home tonight. You're intoxicated. Thank you for the part you played to make my bridal shower successful, but as soon as daylight rises, I want you to leave here. You are no longer welcome here or at my wedding. It will take some time for me to get over your betrayal. Stay away from me, and my family. Please get some help."

"Sasha, you can't do this. I have my wedding gown." That was a slip of the tongue. Tina looked at Sasha with embarrassment.

"And I'm sure you'll get to use it someday, Tina."

"I-I-I meant to say bridal gown."

Sasha stood with a smile, then thanked everyone for coming to celebrate with her. She walked into her room and slammed the door.

The women went back to their partying as Tina lay in a drunken stupor on the floor. Kellie escorted John and Travis out of the suite. The ladies had some shots to help them calm down, but they partied for most of the night.

Sasha

24

T ina was up before everyone. She thought she had a nightmare, but when she woke up in a corner of the living room in the suite, she knew it wasn't a dream. She had opened up to Sasha about her true feelings for John in front of the entire wedding party and other guests.

Tina wanted to quietly go into Sasha's room and beg for her forgiveness. But, when she saw the caterers coming in to make breakfast for everyone, she decided to slip out of the hotel before anyone noticed.

Sasha was up. She went to the window and saw Tina getting into her car. She wanted to get her attention but decided Tina might be too fragile and develop a false hope for their friendship. Sasha stepped back from the window, so Tina wouldn't see her. Then, her phone rang. She was surprised to see it was Michael.

"Good morning," she said.

"Sasha, it's your big day, huh?"

"How did you know?"

"How do you think I know?"

"Tina, of course. I should have known."

There was a brief pause between them, and then they both chuckled.

"So, are you ok, Sasha?"

"You know, Michael, I believe I am. Thanks for asking."

"Well, I just wanted to reach out to wish you all the best on your wedding day. I hope he knows he is a lucky man. Oh, and be sure to let him know if he doesn't treat you right, he will have hell to pay—and I mean that."

Sasha smiled. "Well, I don't think you will have to make good on that promise, but it's definitely nice to know you care."

"I care, Sasha. I always have. I'm sure you're happy, but just know I'm a phone call away if you ever need me for anything."

Sasha swallowed hard. "Well, I guess I better get off this phone and get ready for breakfast."

"Stay sweet, Sasha."

"You, too, Michael."

Sasha hung up and then let out a sigh of relief. She hadn't talked to Michael in months. She didn't know how to share the news of her wedding day with him. Michael seemed to take the news well, and that was all Sasha wanted.

Everyone woke up, starving. They all rushed out to have breakfast. Mrs. Saunders came to have breakfast with the ladies and to check on her future daughter-in-law. Glenn had called his mother earlier and filled her in on the drama from the previous night. Mrs. Saunders wanted to offer Sasha her support.

The ladies sat down to eat at eight A.M., and it was ten o'clock when they came up for air. Kellie was the first to speak.

"We must be out of here at twelve, ladies, but let's get ourselves together, so we can leave at eleven-thirty."

Sasha sat at the table with her head down. Mrs. Saunders slowly walked over to her. "Honey, what's wrong?"

"Did Glenn tell you what happened last night?" Sasha said meekly.

"Yes, dear, he called me this morning."

"Well, I don't have a maid of honor, and now there will be one male looking out of place without a woman on his arm."

"You might not have a maid of honor, but you can have two matrons of honors if you'd like." Mrs. Saunders smiled.

Sasha jumped up and hugged her. "Okay. I'd love that."

They hugged again. "Let's get out of here," Mrs. Saunders told her.

An hour and a half later, Kellie gathered the guests who stayed overnight. "Ladies, we have to get out of here. The limos are waiting for us. We can talk later at the church. We need to get this bride there, so she can get her beauty services."

The make-up artist, the manicurist, and the beautician were all there. Just after Kellie had her makeup done, Travis came downstairs and called her to come out.

"Yo, Kellie, Glenn says he thinks he saw Tina's car in the parking lot. What do you want me to do?"

"Shit. Well, we have to keep an eye on her. Give me a second."

Kellie peeped inside the room and saw Sasha with a glow. She didn't want to disturb her, so she smiled and then gave a slight wave.

"Hey, beautiful. I'll see you upstairs," Kellie told her.

Sasha nodded and smiled at her sister. Kellie closed the door and then followed Travis upstairs.

It was three o'clock at Christ Temple Baptist Church. The ceremony was about to begin. The keyboardist played "Why I Love You" by MAJOR. The male soloist was instructed not to begin singing until he saw Sasha heading down the aisle. The church was full, and all heads turned toward the door, waiting for the beaming bride.

When the door opened, Travis stood there without Sasha. He beckoned for Kellie. Kellie politely slipped out and closed the door. Travis told her Sasha wouldn't come out of the room. Kellie ran down the stairs to Sasha and knocked on the door.

"Sash, are you okay in there? Can I come in?"

"Yes, please come in.''

"Oh, Sash, what's wrong?"

"Girl, I am nervous."

"I don't understand. Why? Don't you love Glenn?"

"You know I do—with all of my heart."

"Then, I really don't get it. Tell me what's going on with you at this moment."

"I feel like the happiest and saddest person in the world. I'm happy to be marrying Glenn, but I'm sad because my best friend is not here."

Sasha began to cry, and Kellie hugged her.

"Stop all of that crying, Sash. You're running your make-up."

Kellie went over to the counter to get some tissue. She returned and dabbed her sister's eyes.

"Sash, this is the biggest step a person can make. You have a handsome man that loves you so much. He's waiting on you. Remember, he is sent by God! Those were your words."

Sasha nodded and then stood. Kellie grabbed her hand and patted it. She also helped Sasha refresh her makeup.

"Come on, Sash. Let's get you married."

Travis waited for them at the door. Once Kellie returned to her place near the altar, the wedding began. The keyboardist never stopped playing, so the song's introduction became the longest one in wedding history.

As soon as the door opened, everyone stood. Sasha and Travis appeared, and the soloist began, causing there not to be a dry eye in the house. Travis led Sasha down the aisle.

Glenn's face was a river. He was so full of joy, he couldn't stop crying even if he wanted to.

All at once, there was a rippling gasp throughout the church. Sasha was concerned at the puzzled faces in the pews as she continued down the aisle. Kellie looked around her sister and saw Tina in a white wedding gown, slowly marching behind Sasha. Kellie was fighting mad. She handed Mrs. Saunders her flowers because this was her final straw with Tina.

Tina suddenly stopped two pews in front of the altar. Sasha turned around to see what was happening. Her head jerked and her eyes widen at the sight of Tina. She was frozen, but her body began to shake as she watched her BFF standing there in a gown that could have very easily been mistaken as a wedding gown.

Glenn took Sasha's hand into his and turned her around to face him. She allowed the first tear to escape down her cheek. Glenn took his handkerchief from his pocket and dapped her face dry.

Sasha turned to look at Tina with eyes that pleaded for her not to make a scene.

Tina smiled at her friend, then turned around and walked back down the aisle. Sasha breathed a sigh of relief. Tina stopped at the doors and turned back to face the audience. She began singing her rendition of Vesta Williams' "Congratulations" song.

The entire sanctuary was filled with loud gasps. Frankly, people were amazed at how beautiful Tina's voice was and stunned at her audacity at the same time. Sasha hadn't heard Tina sing in a long time. Even she had forgotten how beautiful Tina sound.

"Congratulations, I thought it would've been me," Tina continued singing. "Standing there with you. I hope you both will be happy. Congratulations, baby—"

Tina suddenly stopped mid-tune then turned around and pushed the doors open, walking out in grand, runway-like style."

The Pastor cleared his throat and asked for the audience to be seated.

The ceremony continued, and the vows and rings were exchanged. Mr. & Mrs. John Glenn Saunders were officially husband and wife. Their kiss lasted a full sixty seconds. Everyone laughed and clapped with happiness for the couple.

Kellie rushed out of the sanctuary. She looked for Tina but couldn't find her. Tina had disappeared. Tina wanted to see Sasha marry John, but she also wanted to experience how it felt to walk down the aisle to the love of her life. Her experience was half-lived, and she lost her best friend due to all of her antics. However, in her own way, she felt everything was still very worth it. Only time would tell.

Sasha was now a wife. Through it all, she learned when ties unbind, sometimes mending is necessary, as in the case with her sister, Kellie. However, in some instances, when ties unbind, they could very well need to stay that way. Losing Tina would soon become the farthest thing from Sasha's mind as she continued building her life and growing her family with Glenn.

Discussion Questions

1. Did Glenn do the right thing by not sharing what happened with him and Tina?

2. In your opinion, did Michael love Sasha and should she be with him?

3. What is your overall opinion of Sasha? Did your opinion of her ever change by the end of the story?

4. If you were Glenn, would you stay with Sasha after she continued defending her friend? Why or why not?

5. Which characters did you root for and why?

6. How do you feel about Glenn going to dinner with Tina at her parents' home? Was it inappropriate? Why or why not?

7. Which of Tina's actions were extreme?

8. Was Sasha ready for marriage? Why or why not?

9. Is there help for Tina, and if so, should Sasha reconsider their friendship?

10. Are there any love or friendship ties that should remain as left by the end of the story?

Acknowledgments

First giving honor and praises to my Heavenly Father who is the head of my life and home. He has guided me throughout this journey from the first day that I found the transcript.

To Ms. Regina who encouraged me to take the steps to enroll in the English classes at the University Of Memphis, thank you.

To Dr. William Duffy my professor and supporter. I thank you.

When I was giving up and feeling hopeless, my Heavenly Father sent an angel into my life—Bestselling Author, Alisha Yvonne. She's my mentor, advisor, and friend with a heart of gold.

Thank you to my daughters: Jackie, Debbie, and my grandchildren—all of whom are my motivators.

Thank you to my niece Chandra, cousin Patricia Ann and the late Doris Heath for also being my encouragers.

To all of my family and friends near and far, thank you and I love every one of you.

About the Author

Mattie Ward is the author of "When Ties Unbind," her debut title, crafted after finding an unfinished manuscript her beloved daughter began before her premature death. Little did Mattie know that this venture would become a journey she'd grow to love.

After enrolling in several courses at the University of Memphis, Mattie honed her creative writing skills and discovered she enjoyed penning short stories during her classes.

Determined to complete the story her daughter started, Mattie pressed her way, knowing it would be done if it was the Will of God. Her faith kept her going, and she is currently working on future projects.

Mattie is a retired counselor, mother, grandmother, and great-grandmother. She is originally from Patterson, New Jersey, and relocated to Atoka, Tennessee in 2007 with her dog, Theo. Before the Covid-19 pandemic, she volunteered for Mid-South Literacy as a mentor to senior adults who wanted to learn how to read. She also enjoyed volunteering at the Orpheum Theater as an usher.

Look for other works of fiction by Mattie Ward, coming soon. Follow Mattie on social media. You may also email her at WardMa2022@gmail.com.

Made in the USA
Columbia, SC
03 July 2024